SAVING

SN❄W

To Ronie-James,

Never give up!

Best Wishes

Mark

W0006117

SAVING SN❄W

M. A. Howland

CLAYbORN
PRESS

I dedicate this tale to my beloved children.
Without them, life would hold no magic.

Chapter One

E va stared out of the car's window. She couldn't see much, just a slideshow of blurry images replaying themselves. She was more interested in the drops of rain frantically joining others, until the cold winds pushed them out of sight. Her parents had told her she would soon make new friends, but she liked the ones she had already. Why did they have to move, anyway? Her father had said he needed to work in another place, but why so far away?

"Not long now," said Mum excitedly.

Why is she so happy? thought Eva. *Mum is losing her best friends too.*

The car slowed, then pulled off the narrow country lane onto a large gravelled drive. Eva listened as the tyres scrunched over the wet stones, pretending not to care where they were.

"We've arrived!" said Dad, looking around smiling.

Eva continued staring out of the window.

"We've done the right thing, haven't we, Tom?"

"Yes of course, darling. Besides, we had little choice. Don't worry, she will come around."

I won't come around, not ever! thought Eva.

"Come on, let's have a look at our new home, I've heard it even has a princess tower. Let's go and explore!" said

1

Mum eagerly.

"We already have a home, Mum, or have you forgotten already?" Eva replied, tears brimming in her eyes.

"Evangeline!" snapped her father. "You do not talk to your mother like that. Look, I understand it's hard, it's been hard for all of us, but please can we just give it a chance. Besides, it's almost Christmas, you're looking forward to that, aren't you?"

Eva choked back her tears and nodded while staring down at her fumbling hands.

"Get your coat on, poppet, it's a lot colder here in the north than it is in the south," said Mum.

The three of them pulled on their winter coats and zipped them up before opening the car doors. Eva didn't really want to wear her coat; she liked the icy air and enjoyed the way it nipped at her nose.

"Leave the bags, I will get them in a bit. Let's hope the keys Angus sent me are the right ones," said Dad, marching up the drive towards their new home.

Eva shut the car door and looked up at the old, empty house. She wanted to ignore it, as if it didn't exist, but it did. She had never seen a house like this before. She wasn't sure if it looked scary or not. Unlike her old house built with red bricks, this house had been built using large stone blocks, as if sculptured from a small mountain. There were plenty of windows, all of which seemed to be of different sizes and shapes. Many had coloured glass that reminded her of old churches. The long roof sagged in places. Eva imagined hundreds of fat crows roosting on top at night. It was a big, solid looking, and very old house, but it looked interesting too.

"You coming? Hurry or you'll freeze!" joked Mum, walking quickly towards the front steps. Dad was already standing at the front porch wrestling with a large bunch of keys that clinked and clanked.

Eva was about to follow, but a powerful gust of icy air whipped about her. As she pulled her coat in tightly, she heard an urgent voice carried upon the wind.

"Help meeee…"

She spun around, but there was no one there. Eva looked back towards the house. Her parents had already walked through the front door. She was certain she had heard the words, like loud whispering in her ears.

"I'm coming, wait for me!" shouted Eva, startled and a little afraid. Swiftly, she ran across the gravel drive and bounded up the worn front steps.

"Mum, Dad, someone just spoke to me, but I didn't see anyone. Was it you?"

"Slow down, dear, what did you say?" said Mum, hunting around for a light switch.

"Never mind," said Eva, feeling a little embarrassed. "It must have been the wind, it's a lot stronger up here than back home."

Eva closed the heavy front door and peered through the amber coloured glass outside, uncertain of exactly what she had heard.

*   *   *

"Is it today they move in, Angus, the family from down south?" asked Dougall, while being served by McKenzie—the stout innkeeper.

"Aye, and they couldna pick a colder one ta do it either. I'll let them be for now, unless they call. I'll pop over in a couple of days ta see if they've settled in okay," replied Angus, rubbing his clumsy, rough hands together, determined to get some warmth back into them.

"Well, as cold as the north wind blows, if they came here for a white Christmas they'll surely be disappointed. How long has it been now, McKenzie?" asked Dougall, doing his

3

best impression of "Auld Man Winter" after dipping his coarse, ginger beard in white froth from his pint of ale.

McKenzie threw a tea towel over his broad shoulder and splayed his thick, red hands on the polished mahogany counter. "By my reckoning, at least twelve years. Sure we've had a few blizzards here and there, but 'naw like it used to be, eh?" offered the brawny landlord, his ruddy cheeks bulging the more he smiled.

"That may be, but if it gets much caulder than today, it'll matter not if it snows and it'll matter not if you've kept a warm seat for me, I shan't be leaving my hoose except ta fetch more firewood," warned Angus, before finishing up his drink.

"Sure you will, there's a fire here too, you daft, old goat, and nowhere sells ale as fine as Fingle's Inn," said McKenzie, proudly polishing a glass to a deep shine.

Angus looked fondly at the huge fire set in the centre of the old inn. Suddenly, the flames danced wildly against the heavily charred iron back plate, as if responding to his thankful gaze. In truth, Angus had more reason to call Fingle's Inn his home, spending just as much time here as anywhere else, if not more. It was the company he came for; the inn had been the heart of the local community for hundreds of years. Whenever there was cause for celebration, or cause for sorrow, or simply a place for refuge, Fingle's Inn was where everyone congregated. Angus looked around at the good folk he had known all of his life and felt a genuine sense of belonging. He also felt as old as the inn itself, with its crooked oak beams and craggy plaster. There were countless photos and pictures that adorned its interior, each a recording of the villagers' stories caught in time, forever preserved for prosperity. Angus believed you could almost hear the exaggerated tales, the tears and the laughter coming from the very walls if you listened hard enough.

"Hmmm, I cannae argue with your logic, so I guess I'll be seeing you two later then," replied Angus, his smiling eyes twinkling brightly.

Dougall and MacKenzie both laughed as the old gamekeeper collected his jacket and hat from a gnarly oak coat-stand that had stood there as long as the inn had, like an ancient doorman, welcoming the weary and offering a silent farewell to the merry customers. As Angus stepped out into the blustery weather, the door was wrenched free from his clasp, slamming loudly into its frame. *Maybe it will be a white Christmas after all?* he pondered, buttoning up his coat higher—hoping the wobbly top button would hold—and pulling his deerstalker hat firmly over his ears, as the first flakes of snow tumbled through the biting, northerly winds.

Chapter Two

E va watched her parents running around, trying to get the lights and heating working. Dad was fiddling with a large iron box that had something to do with fuses. It looked more like a rusty tool box crammed with dusty wires all jockeying for a position while trying to escape from the irritated intruder, as he tugged and weaved his cold fingers where they weren't welcome.

Mum had emptied some shiny, black coals on the fire grate from an antique copper coal bucket depicting a shire horse pulling along a plough. The fireplace was so large, Eva suspected her mum could stand in it, although her head would probably end up the chimney. After a few scrunched-up balls of newspaper were lit, the flames gradually marched a path across the glittering, gritty coals, which eagerly welcomed their warmth and began glowing red around the edges. The smell was strange to Eva; she'd only had central heating before, but the earthy, sooty scent of burning coal was thrilling and new.

She smiled at the enthusiasm her parents showed for their important tasks. If boring grown-ups were excited, then why wasn't she? Eva already knew the answer and felt for her mobile phone in her pocket, even though she had already checked it a dozen times.

Saving Snow

She supposed her friends were probably too busy to call, to see if she had travelled all the way to Scotland safely. Maybe because they were in another country the phone calls were more expensive? Or maybe they had already forgotten her?

"Eva, we'll do the unpacking later. Let's go and see where we will be sleeping—first come, first served!" said Mum, giggling and running upstairs.

Eva looked up at the staircase; it was enormous. The dark wooden handrail alone looked carved from a single tree. She walked forwards and ran her hand over the cool, dark, polished stair-post, tracing her fingers up its barley twist design. Finally her hand rested upon the solid acorn cap at the top, noticing how the colour appeared lighter, presumably after years of brushing over it. The house was old, very old, but also beautiful. Eva knew nothing of building houses or of carpentry, but she knew enough to appreciate the skill and the love which had been put into the building. She also knew old buildings often held secrets, secrets just waiting to be discovered.

"Coming, Mum!" she shouted, trying not to sound too eager, but her curiosity had gotten the better of her as she leapt up the creaking staircase.

"We're in here, sweetheart," called Mum, from the first bedroom on the landing.

The main thing Eva noticed as she walked in was the smell. It was musty and reminded her of the way her old attic would smell when she would help Dad fetch down the Christmas decorations. The room looked clean enough though, with only a thin layer of dust coating the furniture.

"What do you think?" said Dad.

"It's okay I suppose, bit big though."

Dad laughed, "Yes it certainly is, probably enough room to chase you around!" and jumped to grab Eva.

She didn't try too hard to escape and soon broke out into

fits of laughter.

"See, I knew we could get a smile from you. Hey, while we put on the bed sheets, why don't you go and find your room, there's plenty to choose from."

Smiling, Eva nodded, although it didn't feel like her usual smile. She walked down the long corridor, decorated with wood panelling either side that rose halfway up the walls. Above the panelling, the walls were covered with a faded, scarlet wallpaper, picturing violet thistles that repeated themselves forever, until looking like polka dots in the distance. Eva listened to the floorboards moaning beneath the long tartan rug running the length of the landing. Although threadbare in several places, the colour was still surprisingly bright, with crisp lines of forest-green and denim-blue criss-crossing over a background of rich berry-red.

Pausing to open each door, she soon realised all the rooms looked the same as her parents', only a little smaller. After opening every door, she counted four bedrooms, five including her mum's, and two large bathrooms.

"Mum, didn't you say there was a tower?" shouted Eva, casually opening drawers in the hope of finding something of interest that had been left by the previous owners.

"Yes, you can just about see the top of it from outside. Why, can't you find it?"

"Let *me* check, Ameina, she's probably missed a door." said Dad, sneaking off to explore further.

"Children!" shouted Mum, struggling with a king-size duvet.

Dad and Eva checked everywhere. All the doors along the single corridor had already been opened and searched, yet they found nothing. If there was an entrance, it had to be somewhere else.

"Let me call Angus. If anyone knows, he will. Why don't you unpack your things, sweetheart."

She watched Dad walk back into his room and close the door. *Why did he close the door?* Ever so quietly, Eva tip-toed over to their room—frowning at the complaining floorboards—and lightly pressed her ear to the door.

"Hello, Angus, yes it's me, Tom. Yes thank you, we found it okay. Yes, we found the electric and heating controls too. Can I just ask a quick question, my daughter was wondering how to get into the tower? We can see it from outside the house, but we can't seem to find a way to get in? Oh... I see..."

Eva knew when her father's voice changed that something wasn't quite right.

"Well?" asked Mum, after Dad had finished the call.

"Angus told me the tower was off limits, apparently it's unsafe for children, so the entrance has been sealed off."

"That sounds odd. What does he mean *unsafe*? Is it something we need to know about? What if the weather's getting in, or rats, or something?" said Mum, growing concerned.

"No, it can't be that, or the rest of the house would be rotting if the rain was coming in, and I haven't seen any rats yet, apart from that big one behind you."

"Tom!" squealed Mum, wrapping her arms around herself.

Dad grinned. "Sorry, I couldn't resist it. So, what do we tell Eva? I don't want to give her another reason to feel worse than she already does. Searching for that tower was the first thing she showed any interest for in weeks."

"I know, Tom, but if it isn't safe, she can't go up there."

"Okay, okay, I will tell her later, but don't blame me when she goes all quiet and moody."

Quiet and moody, thought Eva, walking away from their conversation. *I don't care if it's unsafe for children. I'm not a child, I'm almost thirteen and that's a teenager.*

For the remainder of the day, they continued unpacking

without too many grumbles. Eva was happy with her new room; it was much larger than her old one. She adored the antique fireplace. She could make out cherubs and flowers carved into the dark mahogany wood and vines with generous bunches of grapes running down the sides. The thick mantelpiece was a solid slab of white marble streaked with grey. It seemed to her like a puddle of milk that was slowly spreading, but it felt solid, smooth, and cool to the touch. There were dusty logs perched together neatly in the fire's grate ready to be lit, but the heavy radiator already made the room cosy and warm. Judging by the amount of times it had been repainted, Eva wondered if it had doubled its original size. Still, the warm paint smell reminded her of home.

Eva walked over to the window. It was a bay window, curving outwards, and had a rounded bench set within, with hot water pipes running beneath. Several orange cushions were scattered along the bench where she could sit comfortably, gazing out at the rolling hills and green pastures, peppered with slow moving sheep.

She had just taken a hot shower, choosing to watch the night sky slowly take shape, while brushing her honey-blonde hair. The sky's soft pinks and drifting oranges gradually became deeper shades of indigo, beset with a treasure trove of gem-like stars.

"Can I come in, sweetheart?"

"Of course you can, silly!" replied Eva, as her parents peeped around the door.

Eva left the warmth of the window bench and hopped into bed. Although creaky and old, it was comfortable and soft; she supposed it was a bit like her dad, and let escape a small chuckle.

"Good to see you smiling again. I promise you it won't be long before you make new friends," offered Mum, stroking Eva's forehead.

She knew her mum was right, but Eva was still hurting. They *were* her friends, friends she had known all of her life. What if she didn't like her new friends as much, or worse, they didn't like her?

Dad bent down and held her hands. "There's something you should know. I spoke with Angus about the tower, he told me the tower was unsafe and that the door had now been sealed up for our safety. I'm sorry."

Eva pretended she hadn't known about it, and despite looking sad, she had not given up on the matter just yet. She would find out for herself just how unsafe it was...

"Hey, Eva, maybe one day when we have all settled in, we could see if we can make it safe again. I shouldn't think it would take too much work?"

Mum shot Dad one of her looks, a look that meant he shouldn't have said what he had. Mum often looked at Dad in that way.

"I don't know about you but I'm exhausted, it's been a very long day, so without further ado, I bid you a wonder-filled goodnight and see you in the morning, my intrepid, little explorer," said Dad, giving her a big hug.

Eva smiled and kissed them both.

"No, Dad, please leave the curtains, I want to watch the stars come out."

After they had left her room, she switched off her fairy bed lamp. It was heavily chipped and the yellow crescent moon the fairy sat on had a long crack running down its centre, but it made her feel safe. It was a part of her old home and she couldn't bear to get a new one. The last thing she remembered as she snuggled into her duvet was the bright moonbeams stretching across her new room.

Chapter Three

"Shut the door, you old bampot, you'll have us all frozen to death standing in our boots!" shouted Dougall from across the busy bar.

"Awa' n bile yer heid, yer talking mince! You've been warming yer bones, while I've been freezing mine out there," replied Angus, closing the door firmly and stamping his feet on the rugged mat.

"Never mind what this doaty dobber's saying, Angus, unlike him, I'm pleased you braved the weather. Usual?" offered McKenzie, who seemed to be polishing the same glass as when Angus had left earlier.

"Aye, that'll be grand so it will. I'll need something ta warm meself, not getting much warmth from Dougall now am I?" quipped the grizzled gamekeeper.

"How's life been treating you today?" asked McKenzie, pouring out a dark, amber liquid into a short, heavy glass.

"Same old, which is just how I like it. Oh, I did get a phone call from the newcomers," replied Angus, rubbing his bristly chin.

"I suppose they've decided it's too cold and turned tails already," teased Dougall.

"No. It was about the tower."

The landlord stopped polishing his glass and set it down

upon the counter.

"What did they want to know, Angus? What did you tell them?" pressed Dougall, his smile now lost beneath his scruffy salt and pepper beard.

"I told 'em what they needed ta hear, I told 'em the tower was not safe for children."

"Have they found the door? Have they been up there?"

"Stop your blethering, you bawfaced galoot! No, Dougall, they have not found the way in, which is why I didnae say no more, so it stays that way."

"Maybe you should have come clean when they were first interested in travelling up here?"

"Tsk! There's nowt ta talk about. What happened ta the Campbell child is all in the past and that's precisely where it's gonna stay. No point in dragging up that sorry tale and making our new guests all jittery."

Dougall leaned in close. "But, Angus, shouldn't they know about the house?"

"There's nothing ta know, Dougall, it's an old hoose, like every other old hoose. I'm not going ta scare good folk away with ghost stories, am I, cos that's all they are, just stories," said Angus, raising the tumbler quickly to his lips until the contents had vanished.

McKenzie folded his bulky arms and looked up at the pair of them. "Aye, that may be so, but it's not the house that's haunted now is it? It's the tower..."

Chapter Four

Eva's sleep was unsettled. She awoke in a start, her back and forehead damp with sweat. She tried to recall her dreams, but the images were fractured and muddled. She knew they were not particularly nice dreams; they had made her sad and she felt like crying.

She decided to take her mind off it by getting a glass of water, in the hope the feeling would fade completely. Fortunately, her parents were sound asleep as she suspected, after a long day's drive with lots of unpacking. Wearing her unicorn slippers hadn't stopped the ageing wood from creaking and she tried to remember where to avoid treading on the return journey. Placing a hand on the staircase handrail, she crept down slowly, allowing her fingers to brush along the cold, polished wood.

The bottom step was bathed in moonlight that shone through the downstairs windows. Eva was glad for the moon. Instead of a dark, spooky old house, she was seeing a mysterious, enchanting world, where everything appeared as something quite different. Heading towards the kitchen, she listened into the silence. The only sounds were her squeaking foot falls and that of a huffy owl braving the wind outside. It sounded close.

As she entered the kitchen, she was relieved to find it

basking in a silvery radiance. The window blinds had been left up and the almost-full moon was clearly visible. Walking towards the sink, she picked up a glass from the draining board and filled it, cringing at the shuddering moans of the reluctant water pipes. It seemed to her that every part of the house was determined to betray her! Eva drank slowly of the icy water, allowing it to trickle down her throat and dissolve away her recent nightmare. In the pale light outside the window, the overgrown lawn, shrubs, and bare branches of the trees all danced together in the strong winds. Although she felt the night's chill, the imagery outside was entrancing.

Placing her empty glass down, Eva turned to head for the door, but something caught her eye. A thin sliver of light was coming from the larder cupboard. *That's not right! I helped Mum fill it earlier and there were definitely no windows in there,* she thought. Tentatively, she approached, her heart beginning to beat a little harder, despite knowing it was just a silly cupboard full of soup and beans. Instinctively, she held her breath, as she reached for the door and pulled it open.

The strange light seemed to be coming from behind the shelves of tins and cereal boxes. Eva carefully moved the food aside, then took a step back and gasped. The light was coming from a long crack that ran down the back wall behind the shelving and along the top and bottom. It was in the shape of a door; perhaps a hidden door?

"This is it! This has to be the door to the tower!"

"What did you say, sweetheart?" asked Dad wearily, as he entered the kitchen rubbing his eyes.

Eva quickly closed the larder door and switched on the lights. "Hi, Dad, I couldn't find the lights, but they're on now... for you... to see."

"I can see that, thanks," said Dad, squinting against the sudden brightness. "What are you doing up, trouble sleeping?"

"Yes, I mean no. I was thirsty and just needed some water, would you like some water?"

"Thanks for the offer but I can manage. You go back off to bed, poppet, sweet dreams."

"Sweet dreams to you as well," she replied, casting a quick glance over to make sure the light was not visible from the cupboard.

Eva walked back up the stairs, although she felt like leaping up them three at a time! After jumping back into bed, she cosied up wearing a big grin, wondering how she could test out her theory. Even if it wasn't the entrance to the tower, it was an entrance to somewhere and that was exciting enough. She needed time alone to see if she could open the door without her parents around; if they knew about it they would forbid her to enter. But if they didn't know about it, then she wasn't doing anything wrong, not really.

Closing her eyes, she imagined what might lie beyond the cracks of light. Another world perhaps, or the mysterious, dangerous tower, or simply just a broom cupboard. Eva knew deep down it was the tower, it had to be. She would never give up searching for it, ever.

Chapter Five

"Good morning, sleepyhead, how many slices, one or two?" shouted Mum.

"Two please, Mum, can I have some honey as well?" replied Eva, yawning wide as she entered the kitchen.

"Of course, can you fetch it from the food cupboard please?"

Eva froze as memories of her earlier discovery came flooding black. Slowly, she walked over, exactly as she had done only hours before. *Surely Mum doesn't know about the doorway, why else would she allow me near it?* Pulling open the larder door she expected her secret to be revealed, but to her relief there was nothing to suggest it was anything but a larder, at least not during daylight. Eva took longer than was necessary, moving things around, but was unable to see anything behind the shelving, just the old wallpaper displaying fading pictures of salt and pepper pots and butter dishes, all appearing to fall from the sky.

"Here it is, Mum," said Eva, handing over a sticky honey jar. Her fingers peeled away as Mum took it. Did she imagine last night? Was it all just another strange dream?

"Morning, poppet, hope you went back to sleep okay, that water was awfully cold," said Dad, buttoning up his shirt, as he walked over and kissed her head.

It wasn't a dream after all! "Yes, Dad, the water was freezing when it went down, it made my belly cold and I burped up cold air," she quickly replied, calmly licking her sticky fingers, despite her heart racing.

Laughing loudly, Dad agreed. "I'll say, but at least it tastes cleaner up here. Angus tells me it comes straight down from the mountains."

"Don't be silly," said Mum, scoffing at the idea.

"No, really it does. If you look out of the kitchen window, you'll see the pipes leading away from the house and up towards the hills."

Ameina peered out of the window, following Dad's finger until she found it. A moss-covered grey pipe, which handrailed the left side of the garden, disappearing beneath an old, rusted gate at the back fence.

"Well, aren't we posh, we have highland spring water running through our taps," Mum joked.

"Eva, your father and I need to run a few errands in town, we shouldn't be gone too long. You can come with us if you wish, see what's around, or you can stay here."

"Are you sure that's a good idea? She barely knows the house and it *is* a bit prehistoric and a little spooky, at least until we unpack everything and make it our home," said Dad.

"Tom, she's not a baby anymore, she might need some time, you know, to get used to things."

This is perfect, it might be my only chance to find the tower, she thought.

"If it's okay, Mum, I would like to stay and maybe call my friends to see how they are doing?"

"Of course it's okay. Just make sure you get something to eat if we're not back by lunchtime. The food cupboard is fully stocked, you couldn't cram a crack of light between those shelves!"

Eva almost choked on her toast.

When everyone had finished breakfast, Eva offered to

wash up. While sloshing the sudsy, warm water over the dishes, she kept looking back at the larder, wondering if the hidden entrance had somehow vanished like magic. But she doubted magic was even real, especially after that silly magician at her tenth birthday party was bitten by a rabbit he was hiding. Eva became deeply suspicious of anyone calling themselves a magician, wizard or a witch, apart from her old head teacher, Mrs Crabapple. If anyone was a witch she was. She was so sour, it was said milk curdled when she entered a room. Eva reckoned magic was simply a bunch of tricks to deceive the mind, although she believed Father Christmas delivered presents; at least the big ones. She just hoped he knew her new address.

"We're going now, love, keep your phone close by and don't answer the door to anyone, we will be as quick as we can," said Mum blowing a kiss, while Dad started the car outside.

Eva blew one back, sending foamy bubbles everywhere. As soon as she heard the front door close, she wiped her hands on her jumper and ran over to the food cupboard, even before the bubbles had popped on the grey slate flooring. As the car tyres crunched away, Eva flung open the larder door and began taking everything off the shelves, then placing the items on the huge oak table that stood in the centre of the kitchen. She needed to drag over one of the heavy wooden chairs to reach the last two shelves, but after an eternity of frantic reaching, carrying, piling, and stacking, the shelves were finally empty.

Standing back, Eva could see no sign of a door. She walked forwards into the large storage cupboard and peered closely at the wallpaper behind the shelves and still nothing. *I know I saw it. It has to be here somewhere.* She began to doubt herself, then abruptly turned to face the kitchen window and grinned at her excellent idea. She ran over and pulled on the cords that hung from the blinds. After several tugs she found the right one and lowered the blinds until the kitchen became darker. Running back, she stepped inside the cupboard and closed the door behind her...

Just as she had seen last night, a thin crack of light appeared—although much fainter—in the shape of a doorway! No wonder she couldn't see the crack in daylight, it had been wallpapered over, but in the darkened kitchen, the light behind the hidden door was now bright enough to shine through the paper. All she needed was something sharp, then she could make a thin cut along the crack of light that hopefully no one would notice. After wasting more precious time she didn't have to waste, she eventually returned with a pair of craft scissors. Opening the scissors wide Eva began carefully running a single blade across the top. Satisfied she had gone far enough, Eva then followed the outline down the side, stopping just above each shelf and beginning again directly below them. She dearly hoped the paper she couldn't reach behind the shelving wouldn't rip into large tears as the secret door opened. Halfway down, she noticed the paper bulging; it had to be where the latch was. Ignoring it for now, she continued past to cut the rest, having to sit on her knees for the bottom section.

When she was happy she had done what she could, she stood back and surveyed her work. As she had hoped, the slit she had made was practically invisible and if you weren't looking for it, you would never see it. After making a small square cut where she imagined the latch might be, Eva carefully peeled away the faded wall paper and groaned. It wasn't a latch at all, or even a handle; it was a lock, and locks needed keys. The only keys she knew of were the heavy bunch that Angus had given to her dad, but had he taken them with him? If they hadn't removed the front door key from the rest of the bunch, then she had no chance of ever finding a key that worked.

Eva ran over to the small table beside the front door and

punched the air with joy after finding them. Running back to the larder she checked her watch. Her parents had only been away an hour; she still had time. Reaching up to the lock she tried each key in turn, even the ones that looked too big or too small, until at last a "click" clicked.

Eva paused, terribly excited and a little afraid. What if it was dangerous, what if something bad happened? She was all alone without any help. *C'mon Eva, you can do this. You're not a little girl anymore, Mum said it herself, just be careful.*

The door was opening surprisingly easier than she expected—the back shelves were still attached, which made the door heavier. A cold rush of air forced through the opening and startled her, Eva steadied herself and continued opening...

"Hi, sweetheart, we're back."

Mum and Dad, not now! What will I say? Eva slammed the door and locked it quickly—remembering the key she had used—then began placing the groceries back upon the shelves.

"Hi hon—what happened? What are you doing, poppet?" said mum, unable to put her bags on the kitchen table.

"Oh, hi, Mum, I noticed the cupboard was really dusty, I was bored so thought I would do some, you know, dusting."

"That's really thoughtful, you didn't need to do that, silly, but thank you all the same. Here, come and take a look at this jumper, see if it fits?"

That was close, thought Eva, while tugging on a huge, stripy, knitted jumper. It felt a little scratchy and smelt a bit like the house, but it was really warm and Eva was grateful for the gift.

After refusing to let Mum help, Eva replaced everything back as it was. At least she knew she now had the key to open it and that she needn't take anything off the shelves, as the shelves moved with the door. For the rest of the day Eva helped unpack the other boxes and decided that very night, when everyone was sound asleep, she would enter the mysterious tower.

Chapter Six

"That's really thoughtful, thank you, poppet," said Dad, kissing Eva after she had brought them both a large glass of water, setting them down upon their bedside tables.

"Goodnight, Mum, goodnight, Dad."

Eva felt a small pang of guilt, but she had to be certain she wouldn't be interrupted by anyone before she could uncover the tower's secrets. Besides, she had done them a favour; they didn't need to get out of bed now.

As she lay in her own bed, she watched the neon blue numbers on her digital clock change painfully slowly. At one point, she was convinced it had gone back a minute. Eva thought about her friends and how she missed them. She realised it had only been a couple of days, but no one had bothered to text or ring her, not even Eve, her best friend. Grownups were always getting confused with their names as they were so alike. It didn't take long before the two girls discovered it helped them to get away with a lot more mischief!

Time spent in her new house seemed longer for Eva, as everything was different and strange, but still, it *was* only two days. She still loved her friends dearly, even if they were forgetful. She was glad she was on a real adventure; it was hers and hers alone, nobody could take that from her. Gradually, she began to drift off. The desire to sleep was far too irresistible, despite the spine-tingling exploration she had planned.

Fortunately, Mum and Dad's deep snoring had stirred her enough to reawaken during the night. Remembering her quest, Eva was barely able to stop trembling with excitement, as she tied her dressing gown around her and crept downstairs—avoiding the squeakiest floorboards, particularly the spot near her parents' door, where a carpet stain looked like a lion's head, ready to warn everyone of intruders with its creaky roar. Every sound she made seemed frightfully louder than normal and she was certain her parents would awaken, but somehow she managed to make it downstairs unchallenged.

Carefully, Eva picked up the set of keys from off the entrance hall table and plucked them apart in search for the tower door key, using the pale, amber light from the front door window. After some effort, Eva removed the right key and placed the rest back down as quietly as a large bunch of keys could be. *This is it, no backing down now,* she thought, unable to stop herself from shaking as she opened the larder.

The hidden doorway's outline was much brighter now, as the moon's glow from somewhere behind had squeezed through the thin tear she had made. After shuffling a few things around, Eva found the lock, pushed the small key in and turned. She had to catch the door quickly before it swung open wide, the extra weight of the fully stocked shelves made holding the door really difficult. As the door settled against the side shelves, she peered inside...

Eva faced heavily worn wooden steps, steps which immediately spiralled upwards. The moonlight coming down from above was unbelievably bright, as if she were standing outside beneath a full moon on a cloudless night. All the silvery cobwebs shimmered as the cold air from above breathed over them.

Gingerly, she tried the first step. It squeaked, but only a little. Again, up another. She held onto the thin, spiralling iron rail; it felt bitterly cold. A procession of murky mirrors—that had rusted along their inside edges—spiralled upwards with the handrail. Eva peered into the mottled antique glass. She looked a ghostly green and watched as more of her breath appeared with every step she climbed. Rising higher, she felt her crown and ear tips begin to freeze with the chilly air funnelling downwards. Upon reaching the sixth circle of spiralling upwards, Eva could see the staircase was ending, to become what must be the entrance to the tower. She fought down an urge to run the last few steps and continued cautiously.

The first thing she observed when entering the tower was the enormous domed ceiling, built entirely from large panes of glass. A cluster of ivy creepers outside clung to the grubby windows like a giant skeletal hand forever seeking a way in. Peeling white paint, hanging all along the window frames, had been urged to let go by the howling drafts and then caught again by the hundreds of cobwebs, as if snowfall had been suspended in time.

Awestruck, Eva walked to the tower's centre. She shivered uncontrollably as the temperature was now freezing, yet, so spellbinding this dreamlike vision, she barely felt its bitter embrace. Like the ceiling, the room was completely surrounded by large windows, allowing anyone to see in any direction. This explained the light reaching downstairs. Light during day or night was free to shine through from one side to the other without any obstruction. As she turned she felt something beneath her foot. Peering down, she noticed what looked like a child's toy, a small, carved wooden dog. She knelt and picked it up; as she did so, across the far side of the room she saw a large object draped in a spectral white sheet and approached it nervously.

Don't be afraid. It's only a bed or something. You can do this. You wanted an adventure. Well, Eva, here it is!

Pinching the corner of the dusty sheet, Eva slowly peeled it away. Another sheet beneath revealed itself, as did a well-loved teddy bear that was tucked up with odd eyes sewn on, one ear missing, and looking absurdly irritated for being disturbed. *This was a child's room, but why has someone left a teddy bear here? Why tuck it up in bed, only to leave it?* wondered Eva, as she pulled back the sheet further to lift the bear free.

Suddenly, an icy blast of air blew across the bed making her jump. Then a strange scraping noise filled the whole of the tower. She heard it crawl around her, spreading, like a frozen lake slowly cracking itself apart. Then she saw the glass. It was frost, only not like any she had seen before. It was increasing its flowery, serpentine advance at an unnatural speed, until it smothered the entire tower. Although losing some of its intensity, the saturating moonlight was still bright, illuminating the frosty, iridescent branches that swarmed upon the panes of frozen glass. The effect was jaw-dropping and although afraid, Eva was captivated by the beauty of the intricate design and how the soft light would stream through in an endless expression of different sparkling colours.

"Help meee... find Snowww..."

It was the same voice she had heard when she first arrived! She was about ready to bolt, but somehow, from somewhere, she found the courage to stay. Eva reasoned that if the same voice had anything to do with the magnificent window frost paintings, then how could it be bad?

"Who are you and what do you want from me? Why do you want it to snow?" she replied shakily, feeling the quaking words tumble from her as if they were not her own.

"Pleeease find her... little tiiiime left..." breathed the anxious, unearthly voice.

Without warning, the frost withdrew from a single window.

"Looook..."

Entranced, Eva walked mechanically towards the clear window, still clutching the bear and breathing sharply. She felt like crying, she felt like calling out for help, but she *had* to look outside. Eva now stood close enough to see her breath misting up the glass. She wiped it away with her sleeve and peered through. It was the same view as from the kitchen: the lawn, the swaying trees that lined the garden, and the tall back fence, all illuminated in otherworldly light.

"What is it? What do you want me to see?" stammered Eva, now crying and feeling like she might unravel at any moment.

"Looook..."

Eva wiped her eyes with her shaking hands and stared harder through the glass, until she saw something move at the bottom of the garden. She leaned in closer, blinking away her tears. Standing at the rusted, back gate stood a small boy staring directly at her, holding the same tattered, one-eared teddy bear.

"Impossible..." was all Eva could manage.

The boy looked deeply sad and quite lost, but there was something more; he looked paler than the platinum light that shone down upon him. The strange boy opened his mouth and spoke, never once removing his enchanting gaze from hers.

Eva couldn't hear anything of course, but as the strange boy spoke, ghostly letters immediately formed in frost upon the glass before her very eyes! Eva dropped to the floor, while watching the words "HELP US" scrawled across the dirty window by some unseen hand...

She ran screaming from the tower, from the mysterious, troubled boy, and from the scary voice with its mystifying frost patterns that continued to fill her mind with its creepy, scraping sound, then promptly slipped down every step until she tumbled into the kitchen.

"What's happening, where are you, Eva, are you alright?" shouted Dad, bursting into the kitchen.

Eva sat sobbing beneath the kitchen table, refusing to open her eyes. Tom bent down and pulled her into his arms, stroking her clammy hair until her breathing slowed.

"What is it, poppet, what happened? You're freezing!"

Still quivering and unable to look up, Eva pointed towards the tower door.

Chapter Seven

Holding her breath, Eva remained as still as possible. She stood outside the kitchen and listened to the conversation her parents were having over breakfast.

"I understand that, Tom, but she has never done anything like this before."

"She has never left all of her friends and moved to another country before. Just give her time, it's a big thing."

"Do you know, not one of her so-called friends has called her yet to see how she is. She is better off without them," said Mum, hastily draining the last of her coffee.

Eva pulled out her phone and looked at the display. Only Eve had texted—which cheered her up—but no one else had. *Mum's right, I am better off without them. Apart from my best friend, the rest don't seem to care. Besides, I'm busy with stuff here, amazing stuff. I'm going to find out who that boy is, if I'm ever allowed to go out again.* As she stuffed her phone back in her jeans, it slipped and fell.

"Eva, is that you?"

The kitchen door opened and Eva shuffled in, head low and looking miserable.

"Our intrepid explorer has arrived," mocked Dad.

"Tom!"

"Sorry, sweetheart. Eva, your mum and I have been talking, we are worried about you. I know this move has changed everything and I know you never wanted it to happen, but we had no other choice, what with my work. However, this does not mean you get to hide things from us, things that could have been dangerous, do you understand?"

Eva nodded and stole a sorrowful glance upwards.

"I'm sorry I should have told you. I wanted an adventure, to... you know, to forget things, I guess," she replied quietly, feeling her cheeks redden and eyes fill up.

"We're sorry you couldn't turn to us. We're not monsters, love, we just care for you, a lot. And you don't have to forget things, your past is a part of you and you should be proud of it. I am proud of who you have become and that's because of your past," said Mum, smiling and holding out her arms.

"I won't go into the tower ever again, I promise," sniffed Eva, walking into her Mum's embrace.

"Good girl. Your father is going to call Angus to have it boarded up properly, aren't you, Tom."

"Eh? Oh, yes, yes of course," replied Dad, giving Eva a wink.

She returned the smile, despite feeling upset about the tower being off limits. Still, what of the strange boy? He still had to be out there somewhere.

"Hi, Angus, it's Mr Landhow, Tom, yes. Yes thanks, were settling in fine, yes I did manage to find the village okay. Yes, everything is working just fine." Dad rolled his eyes. Eva stifled a laugh. "I'm actually calling about the tower... hello? Are you still there, Angus? Sorry, I thought the phone call had cut off. No, I'm afraid my over-curious daughter found the entrance. I had a quick look myself and it looks dangerous up there, you can hear the wind rattling the glass about the rotting frames. Yes, that would be splendid. Eva? Hold on." Tom placed his hand over the mouthpiece. "Sweetheart, Angus wants to talk with you quickly, to make sure you're okay."

Eva screwed up her face. *What does he really want to know?* she thought.

She took the phone from her dad after he put it on loudspeaker and drew in a quick breath. "Hello?"

"Hello, am I speaking ta wee Eva?"

"Yes, that's me."

"Good, good. I heard you found the tower, all by your canny self, now that takes some doing! Now, you know that place was locked up for a reason, it's unsafe ta go rambling in the ramparts, too much glass and not enough glue. When that cauld wind comes howling over the hills, it rattles anything it touches, including ma knobbly, knocking knees, even when I'm not wearing ma kilt. I'm going ta have ta board it up properly, it's for your own safety, lass."

"That's okay, I understand. I'm very sorry for causing you any trouble, Angus."

"It's nay bother, it will give me a reason ta come pay you a wee visit. Now before I go, is there anything you want me ta bring, anything you need?"

Eva looked towards Mum and Dad; they both smiled and shook their heads.

"No it's fine, we have everything we need, thank you, Angus. Oh, can I keep the teddy bear before you board up the tower please?"

"What teddy bear, lassie?"

"The little boy's bear, Harry's bear."

"Yes... yes of course you can... Tell your maw and da, I'll be round later, bye for now."

Eva handed her father's phone back after the call had finished. Carrying the tattered bear, she disappeared back up to her room.

*   *   *

"What is it, Angus? Who was that, the newcomers over at old Campbell's place?" asked McKenzie, studying his old friend closely.

Angus nodded slowly and tucked his phone away.

"Well, you look like you've seen a ghost, what did they say?" pressed Dougall.

"It's their wee bairn, she found the tower so she did. They want me ta come round and board it up properly ta stop her going up again," muttered Angus, heading for the pub door.

"Well, that's a good thing isnae? At least she won't find out about the Campbell boy."

"She already knows."

Dougall and McKenzie looked at each other. Dougall spoke first. "Angus, dinnae worry yourself, if you're boarding it back up properly, once and for all, that'll be an end to it and the troubles won't happen again."

Angus pulled on his hat and reached for the door handle without looking back. "I'm afraid it's too late, it's already happening. The lassie knows the Campbell boy's name, how do you think she found out when I didnae tell 'em? That can only mean one thing: he's back, *Williwaw's* come back..."

Chapter Eight

"Mum, can I go out and fetch some holly and berries? I thought we could make some decorations. It's Christmas Eve tomorrow, after all," asked Eva hopefully.

"Hmmm, it's awfully cold out there, the wind has really picked up."

"I can wear that new woolly jumper, it'll be like wearing a heated radiator. If it's good enough for sheep, I will be just fine."

"Okay, I suppose a little fresh air can't hurt, but don't stray too far please, if the weather takes a turn for the worse I want you close by."

Eva kissed her mum and grabbed her coat. Slamming the back door, she bounded down the steps and ran into the blustery garden. She recalled her dream from last night after running from the tower. It wasn't a bad dream, not frightening at all, just strange. She remembered seeing the boy and he told her his name was Harry. He said he was searching for snow and needed Eva's help desperately. He told her that if she went through the gate at the bottom of her garden, he would be waiting for her...

The sky was overcast with an odd pinkish hue. In the dim light, Eva could see her mother reading a book next to the open fire. She didn't think that going through the gate would be going too far, but still, she checked she was not being watched as she slipped through the rusty opening. There was a simple pathway which the bracken and brambles tried in earnest to conceal. Almost immediately it had taken a sharp bend away from the back garden and led up into the hills. Occasionally, large, slippery rocks would need clambering over, but by the look of things, much of the wildlife continued to use the trail, which had made it easier to climb the steep slope.

Looking back, the house became smaller the farther she climbed. She remembered her mother's parting words and almost turned back, but she could now see the top of the hill where an ancient yew tree sat, lonely but welcoming. *I will just sit by the tree, I can still see the house, it will be fine,* thought Eva.

A little out of breath, she sat upon a large stone jutting out from the ground, smothered in vibrant moss with streaks of brilliant white quartz running through, that occasionally sparkled in the low light.

"Hi."

Eva jumped up and almost fell backwards! Standing before her was Harry, the strange boy she had seen standing at her gate from the tower *and* in her dreams, who seemingly appeared from out of thin air.

"Harry, you scared me! Where did you come from? I should have seen you coming, I thought you would be waiting at the gate?" stammered Eva, backing away a little.

"Sorry, I didn't mean to scare you. I waited at my gate but didn't see you, so I figured you might walk to the top of Hollow Hill. I'm glad you came to help me, Eva."

"How did you know my name?"

"Last night you told me, don't you remember?"

"Not really. I remember some of my dream, you were in it. Did you dream the same dream?"

"Yes. I think children can do it better than grownups."

"This is cool and a little weird. Hey, why do you look so sad anyway? Is it your bear, because I found another one in the tower? Was that your room before we moved in?" said Eva, feeling a little more relaxed.

"You mean *is* my room. No, I haven't lost my bear, I still have it. It's not being able to find Snow that makes me so sad."

That was an odd thing to say, thought Eva, *maybe he isn't ready to let go of his old room just yet?* Eva knew how hard it was leaving her old house; it was more than just a building, it was her home.

"Snow? As in the snow that falls in winter?"

"Yes! And no..."

"I don't understand, Harry. Can you tell me more, then maybe I can help?"

"Yes. One night, when I first slept in the tower it got really cold, freezing and then it began to snow. I jumped out of bed and looked outside, then I saw the frost, it was everywhere."

"I saw that too! It made gorgeous patterns all over the glass, really, really quickly," replied Eva, her chocolate brown eyes wide with excitement.

Harry nodded. "I got a little scared and asked who was doing it, then I heard the wind talk."

"I heard it too, it's a man's voice inside the wind, isn't it."

"Yes. He told me his name is Boreas. I asked him why he doesn't show himself, he said he was too weak to do it anymore because of losing Snow. Snow is his daughter's name."

"No way! Is he a ghost or something? Is Snow a ghost too?"

"No. Boreas said they come from far away, a place called Hyperborea, I think?"

35

"This is amazing, Harry! I can't wait to tell Mum and Dad, that's if they'll believe me."

"No! You mustn't. We do not have any time left, they will not believe you, grownups never believe."

Eva looked at Harry thoughtfully, then back towards her new home. Even at this height she could still see the warm glow of the fireside in her living room. "Okay, I won't say anything, for now. So where do we start looking then?"

Harry jumped in the air waving his arms, it was the first time she had seen him smile.

He eagerly explained where he had already searched, directing her gaze with a sweep of his hand. It was a vast area, covering hills, fields, and valleys.

"How long have you been looking?" gasped Eva, shocked at the distances.

"You know, it's funny, I can't exactly remember?"

"Well, has it been months, or longer perhaps?"

"It feels like only yesterday, but it must be longer, I think...?" Harry seemed lost again and his bottom lip began to quiver.

"It doesn't matter, Harry, I'm here now. We shall find Snow together, I promise."

The Campbell boy looked up with a crooked smile. "Thank you, Eva, I can feel her close by, she feels afraid and very sad I think."

"How close? You've looked everywhere, what's left?"

"There's one place I can't go, I have tried, many times, but I'm too afraid."

"Where?"

"Further down the hill and to the left. See that old building, the one with the big stone wall all around it, there might be a way in somewhere, but I can't remember where it is? I keep forgetting things... When I walk around it I think I can feel Snow somewhere inside, but I don't think we can get in."

"Let's go and save your Snow, then, Harry."

The two rescuers carefully made their way down the steep slope, ever closer towards solving the mystery but further away from Eva's home. The decline was littered with wet stones pushing up from long sodden grass. At one point, a small stream lay across their path and they were forced to find a narrower part to leap over.

"Tell me more about Snow's dad, Harry."

"Boreas?"

"Yes."

"Well, we all know him around here as Williwaw, but you might know him as Jack Frost."

"Yes! I've heard of Jack Frost, but I never knew he had a daughter."

"Neither did I, until he told me. When he used to be stronger, I could almost see him, but as the snowfall got less and less, so did his strength. Now I can only hear him."

"Why is that?" asked Eva, jamming her cold hands tightly into her jacket pockets.

"Boreas told me his daughter is the reason it snows and without her we wouldn't have any. She creates snowflakes in her own world and then they fall into ours. He said that one day his daughter Snow wanted to see what it felt like to be a falling snowflake, so she became one and tumbled downwards from her world into ours. That was the last Boreas ever saw of her. He knows she's still alive somewhere, but they both grow weaker every time Boreas looks for her."

"Why is that?"

"Boreas said, because his daughter's trapped here, all the snowflakes from his world are running out and without his daughter, no more snowflakes can be made to come here. And every time he enters our world, it becomes so cold it snows, so now he's afraid to search for her because if the last snowflake falls before he can find her, she will die! But if he doesn't come into our world, his daughter will not have the strength to leave without him, that's if he ever finds her."

"And it will never snow again?" murmured Eva.

Harry nodded, looking down at his scruffy shoes.

"We *must* find her, Harry."

Harry smiled, wiping his nose on his sleeve. The small boy led Eva to the old stone wall. It was much higher than they were and looked like it had been there forever.

"Sometimes, Harry, all you need is another pair of eyes. If you search that way, I will go this way and hopefully we will meet somewhere on the other side."

Harry nodded hesitantly and disappeared into the swirling fog.

There is always a way in. You just have to search for it, she thought.

Eva began trudging through the rebellious winter ivy, and sidestepped wayward bramble patches as she traced the ancient route. The stone wall was heavily pitted, with large orange patches of peeling lichen that looked like decorators had lost their brushes halfway through painting it. Eventually she arrived at the corner bend and looked back. Most of what she had just walked was now lost to a ghostly shroud of tiny rain droplets that churned and swirled in the night air.

One wall down, three to go...

It was darker along this side, and for the first time since leaving the house, she began to feel afraid. The world had become eerily quiet. Without realising, Eva began creeping along the boundary path. She tried to keep her presence unknown for fear of disturbing a Highland beast lurking somewhere within the misty grasses, ever ready to pounce upon unwelcome newcomers. Staring into the white abyss, Eva bumped against an old, rusted plough, disturbing a string of crows that leapt from off the stone wall, demonstrating their outrage in echoing, raspy cries before dissolving into the fog completely.

She leaned hard against the wall—which was besieged with prickly gorse—while catching her breath. Eva winced at the thorns stabbing through her jacket, but daren't move until her heart had stopped thumping. When she heard nothing but the unconcerned sheep and wailing winds, she bravely resumed.

Not a single sign of entry was found anywhere within the walls she walked past. Eva began to believe that Harry may have been right all along. After searching along three sides without any luck, Eva cornered the final bend and was nearly thrown off balance as a powerful gust of wind forced her backwards. Tilting her body into the wind and keeping her head down, she continued onwards.

This is silly, I will find a way in, there has to be one. I should have met up with Harry by now. I hope he's okay. Maybe he's already found a way in?

It was hard to see anything through the thick fog and screaming winds, winds which were driving tiny beads of freezing rain hard against her small frame, stinging her eyes and numbing her face. If it hadn't been for the sudden gust that pushed her back, she would never have seen the entrance gate hidden behind the swaying ivy. Pulling ruthlessly against the clinging plants that seemed desperate to deny her entry, Eva discovered a latch and pulled on it. The latch had not been used for a long time and she needed to lean against the blistered, corroded metal with all of her weight, until eventually it opened, just enough for her to squeeze through.

Immediately everything became calm. The violent wind remained largely outside; only its deep, whistling rumble could still be heard. Eva surveyed her new surroundings. It was an old, abandoned churchyard.

"Harry! Harry, where are you?"

Eva stood motionless waiting for a reply. The only sound came from a braying animal somewhere beyond the wall, which was soon lost to the urgent wind.

Well, I shall have to go looking myself, shan't I. Boys are always bragging about what they're going to do and can't be found when it comes to doing it! complained Eva. Mum often said as much about Dad, she thought.

Something quite unexpected happened the moment her foot stepped forwards. A flurry of soft snowflakes began falling around her and increased quickly in speed. Eva had only seen snow fall once, several years ago, and then it hadn't lasted long enough to settle, but this... this was *very* different. The sudden heavy snowfall made seeing much more difficult and combined with the freezing fog and powerful gales that had suddenly returned, it was practically impossible to see any further than where she was placing each foot.

"Harry! Are you here? Please help me!"

Eva was uncertain which way to turn, constantly tripping over knotted tree roots and neglected, fallen headstones of long-forgotten buried townspeople. Everywhere she looked, a shifting veil of white was all that could be seen and this gradually became greyer as the fading daylight left the valley, to be replaced by rapidly dropping temperatures.

What have I done? Why didn't I listen to Mum? What if I can't ever find my way back home?

Eva collapsed in a heap and began to cry. She had never felt so alone and helpless. She had left her friends, left the home she had dearly loved and grown up in, and left her parents, parents who only ever loved her. They weren't trying to ruin her life, but were instead trying to do the best they could for her. She had known this all along and sobbed harder as the snow built around her, numbing her chilled, tired body to the point where she began to feel drowsy.

"Youuu are neveeer alone, child... wake uuuup, wake uuuup..."

Eva opened her eyes and blinked away the snowflakes,

as the strange voice lingered in her mind.

"Boreas, is that you?"

"Yessss..."

Shaking the sleepiness from herself, Eva got back onto her feet and began stamping life back into her frozen toes.

"I *will* find Snow, she's here somewhere, isn't she?"

"Yessss..."

Hugging her shivering body, Eva moved forwards and kept on moving, until a powerful gust of wind pushed her to the left.

"Is it this way, Boreas?" She coughed, as icy flakes fell into her mouth and danced around her eyes.

"Yessss..."

Encouraged by the help from Snow's father, Eva kept pushing on through the furious blizzard. Every couple of feet she either fell or slipped, completely blinded and increasingly fearful. She couldn't tell if she had been stumbling around for a minute or for an hour, having lost all sense of time in the frozen wilderness. What if something terrible happened to her? What if her parents couldn't find her before it was too late? Even if a search party would dare risk a rescue in this weather, no one would know where she was. Eva began to cry again. She was exhausted and frightened and was very close to giving up.

"Keeeeep going, Evaaaa..."

"I ca— I can't..."

Sobbing uncontrollably, little Eva collapsed for the second time, wishing she had never gone on such a stupid quest. She dearly wished she was back home with her mum and dad, eating Mum's sizzling pancakes while Dad drizzled the maple syrup, holding the bottle up ridiculously high and getting it everywhere.

Curled up with her eyes closed, she felt the soft flakes gently settle upon her head and realised the winds had now died down. Slowly, peacefully, she opened her eyes. In the twilight, something caught her eye. It was a dim, whitish glow that seemed to come from somewhere in the ground up ahead.

"Snowwww..."

After hearing Boreas call his daughter's name, Eva found the strength and climbed back onto her feet once again. Staggering towards the pale light, she watched it become brighter with every clumsy stride she took, until she arrived at some steps leading underground. The steps ended abruptly where another gate stood. Mesmerised by the soft light, twinkling somewhere beyond the opening, Eva took her first step down the icy stairs and slipped, falling into a crumpled heap after her head struck the iron gate heavily.

"Evaaaaaa... Evaaaaaa..."

Chapter Nine

"Of course I tried her phone, she didn't take it with her!"

"Well, what did she say before she left?"

Eva's mother turned to Tom, still shivering from the cold. "She said she was collecting berries for Christmas decorations, I said fine and told her not to stray too far. I did, Tom, honestly I did. Then after twenty or so minutes, I looked out of the window but couldn't see anything, so I went to the back door and shouted after her."

"How long ago was this exactly?"

Holding up a shaky watch to her swollen eyes, Ameina replied, "Almost two hours ago. I went outside after I called for her and looked around the garden. I found the gate at the bottom had been left open, so I went through and started calling, but nothing."

Eva's mum broke into tears, Tom bent down and held her. "It's not your fault, love, we'll find her, she can't have gone too far. She is probably lost somewhere in this crazy snow. I will call Angus, he will know what to do and who can help."

*　　*　　*

"What is it, Angus? You look like you've seen a ghost," said Dougall, watching the old gamekeeper lower his phone with his unblinking eyes still fixed upon it.

Slowly, Angus looked up. All colour had drained from his face. "It was the newcomers, down at Campbell's place. It's their daughter, she's gone missing..."

The regulars all looked over when McKenzie dropped a crate of empty bottles. "Is this a joke?" he stammered, oblivious to the broken glass.

Looking much older than he should, Angus cleared his throat. "I'm afraid it's no joke. The bairn's been missing for two hours."

"In this weather! The last time we had snow this bad was when—"

"Was when the Campbell boy disappeared, I know," finished Angus, watching the despair spread over Dougall's face.

"We're going to need a team for—" began Angus, rising from his stool, then almost collapsed.

Dougall rushed over and helped him back onto his seat. "Angus, it won't happen again! We *will* find her. Just take a wee moment to gather yourself."

"We don't have a moment!" spluttered the gamekeeper, his eyes welling up as painful memories of searching for young Harry flooded his frantic mind.

"I'll assemble a search party and call Owen down at the police station, he will get us extra help. Just take it easy on yourself, old man, Harry was *never* your fault and like you say, we'll find the girl," said McKenzie, pouring out a drink for his trembling friend.

"Aye, you're right, lad, I know you're right, but we need ta move fast before Williwaw takes another child from us."

Within minutes the landlord had everyone outside. Those that could not get into vehicles bravely trekked through the blizzard, heading down towards the Campbell residence, wrapped up and carrying torches. It was tough going, the snowfall was unrelenting and in some places the windstorm had whipped it up to waist-high depths.

Tom opened the front door before Angus had walked down the drive.

"Thank God you've arrived, thank you for coming."

Angus nodded and managed a smile. "It's the least we can do, we look out for each other when we can. Tell me, where was the last place your wee lass was seen?"

"The back garden, my wife tells me the rear gate was left open."

"Aye, likely she wandered up Hollow Hill and back down the other side into the valley. In this weather she probably got lost. Try not ta worry, Tom, we all know these parts very well."

"I'm coming too!" yelled Ameina, buttoning up her coat.

"Sweetheart, I need you here. If Eva comes back home someone will need to be here for her, she will be frozen half to death and most likely terrified."

Ameina was about to protest then agreed.

Tom kissed his wife. "If she comes back here, call me or Angus straight away so we can stop the search." Ameina nodded, wiping her eyes. "Look at me, Ameina, I *will* find our daughter!"

"I know..."

*　　*　　*

Ameina watched as the brave party walked up the hill, obscure figures with dull sweeping torch beams that lanced into the night, eventually becoming swallowed up by the churning whiteness.

Please, God, help her, help my little Eva.

A strong gust rattled the kitchen windows and Ameina opened her eyes, allowing trapped tears to fall into the dishwater. She stared in amazement while beautifully intricate frost ferns smothered the entire window at an impossible speed. But before the frost met in the centre, an iridescent word unfurled before her disbelieving eyes...

*   *   *

"Hold on, Angus, it's Ameina, maybe Eva's back home!"

The gamekeeper studied Tom's face while he spoke to his wife.

"Angus, is there a churchyard anywhere near here?"

His eyes widening, Angus nodded. "Aye, there is, only a short way from here, it's been abandoned for many years, why do you ask?"

"My wife says we need to search a churchyard. I know, it doesn't make much sense to me either, but she seemed certain."

"Not much does these days! Well, seeing as there's one over yonder, we best go looking anyway."

Tom agreed and the party increased its pace, calling and shouting for little Eva as loudly as possible. Several of the group used rescue whistles, but the raging storm mercilessly devoured all other sound.

After a perilous descent, they moved further away from Hollow Hill and closer to the bleak, formidable wall that kept hidden the old abandoned churchyard.

"How do we get in?"

"There is a way, but if I'm honest, as far as I know no one's been in here for a right smart spell. Folk don't like ta bother the dead and there's been no shortage of ghost stories in this valley."

"We'll split into two teams, Angus," hollered McKenzie. "We will go this way and your team go the other."

After what seemed an unbearable length of time, the two teams finally met up with each other.

"We can't find any entrance, there has to be one somewhere!"

"This is no good, we can't be wasting precious time like this, where's Tom?"

In the dim light and poor visibility no one had seem Tom disappear from the group.

"Quick, we must turn back the way we came, maybe he's found a doorway, or maybe he's found his daughter?"

"Maybe he's lost too?"

"I can't even begin ta think like that, we must move quickly!"

Fearful that Eva and now her father were lost to the storm, the search party hastened their efforts by spreading out as far as they dared, searching desperately along the gloomy enclosure and desolate grounds.

"Over here!"

Dougall had found Tom's torch. It had been propped up in the snow, still shining and pointing towards a rusty gate obscured by ivy.

"He's found a way in and gone on alone. Quick, bring everyone inside!" shouted Angus, feeling hope rekindle within his aching heart.

* * *

"Eva... Eva!" Tom wandered blindly amongst the broken headstones, calling out his daughter's name, while thoughts raced around his panic-stricken mind. *I wish we had never moved. My little Eva was right. How foolish I was to think it was the best for all of us, how selfish. I am so sorry Eva... please come back to us.*

Stumbling around blindly in the snow, Tom craned his head to one side as he heard the faint, yet distinct barking of a dog. It didn't sound too far away. Staggering through the grave yard, he continued following the excited yelps until several figures blurred into view.

"Tom? Is that you? Tom, quickly, we've found your daughter."

Tom fought to get closer, battling against the snow and ice, afraid of what he might discover.

"Let me through, is she alright?"

"Aye she's alive, frozen, but alive the poor, wee thing. McKenzie's wolfhound had just found her, she was lying at the entrance ta the crypt. Looks like she slipped down the steps and banged her head. In some ways she was lucky, at least down there she managed ta keep out of the worst of the storm."

Tom ran down the steps, despite nearly slipping over and picked up his shivering daughter.

"Sorry, Dad, really I am, I was looking—"

"Shhh, you just save your strength, poppet, I will get you home as quickly as I can and make you a huge mug of hot chocolate."

"With squirty cream?"

"Yes, yes of course!" laughed Dad, rubbing his eyes with the back of his glove. "Hush now, we can talk later."

Eva nodded, managing a weak smile as she snuggled in closer.

The walk back was a little easier. The storm had thankfully eased, considerably so, and visibility was much improved. Eva felt strong enough to walk beside her father but still kept in close. As the band of brave rescuers walked down the hill approaching the rear garden, Eva's house was completely lit up. Its warm glow cast over the glittering, deep snow that had fallen that evening. Ameina ran out to meet them, wrapping Eva in a huge blanket she had been keeping warm by the fireside.

*   *   *

The old gamekeeper watched the weary couple lead their daughter back inside their new home, then thanked all the villagers who came out to help, every one of them courageous and compassionate as any good soul could be. As they left, tired but high spirited, Angus watched his friends vanish back towards their own homes. *It's times like these I feel truly honoured ta be part of such a wonderful community,* he thought warmly, with a lump in his throat.

"Thank the heavens, thank *you*, Angus, and thank everyone else in this village. I can't imagine what she was doing out there and in this weather. It makes no sense!" said Tom.

Angus smiled, entered, and closed the front door, stamping his heavy boots on the mat. "Nay trouble, we look out for each other around these parts, especially when the weather takes a turn for the worse. Rest assured, ol' Williwaw will not take another child on my watch!"

"Another child?"

Angus coughed his discomfort, then walked into the living room to stand by the fire where Ameina was rubbing warmth back into Eva's frozen limbs. "There's something you should know, something maybe I should have mentioned about the hoose. There was good reason the tower was sealed up. The family who lived here before never had any problems, that is until their wee boy began using the tower for his bedroom."

The gamekeeper's face took on a hard edge as the firelight framed his serious eyes. "The young laddie was convinced the tower was haunted."

Suddenly, a shrieking howl of cold air whooshed down the chimney startling everyone, sending red sparks and billowy, grey smoke into the fireguard.

"There's a local legend that tells of a restless spirit who searches out children, to then steal them away by leading them into a snowstorm. We call him *Williwaw*."

"Nonsense! I don't appreciate this kind of talk, you are scaring our daughter!" chided Tom, as he grabbed Angus's coat sleeve and began walking him to the front door.

"Stop! It's okay, Dad, really it is. Please let him stay, I want to hear the rest of his story," pleaded Eva, cradling her hot mug of chocolate.

"I'm sorry, Tom, I never meant any disrespect. I am just trying ta explain the troubles we have had and I thought it important ta tell you everything."

Ameina looked at Tom and nodded. "It's okay, Angus, it's been a difficult night for everyone, we would appreciate it if you continued," she said smiling.

"Right you are, lassie. Several years ago a young family, like yourselves, moved into this very hoose, and they had a wee girl about Eva's age. One night, just like tonight, that little girl went missing too, but fortunately we found her before it was too late. She was blundering around in a dreadful snowstorm calling out for snow."

Tom spoke up, "You mean she wanted *more* snow?"

"It would seem that way, almost as if she wanted the snow to overcome her, ta take her from this world maybe?" said Angus, scratching his bristly cheek.

Eva was about interrupt then thought better of it. *They don't know the whole truth, but I do...* she thought.

"Well, the wee lass claimed someone made her do it, spoke ta her, convinced her ta go out in the storm. That someone is who we all call Williwaw. The family moved away shortly after that, then the Campbell family moved in. I didn't see any point in telling them what had happened. After all, who is ta say the girl was even telling the truth, or maybe she was a little unwell or something. So, as I said, the Campbell's young boy decided ta make the tower his bedroom. Not long after that he went missing too."

"Did he go missing during a snowstorm?" asked Ameina, concern etched into her face.

"Yes."

Everyone looked down at Eva. She grew uncomfortable very quickly and needed the focus shifting elsewhere. "But you found Harry too, didn't you? Was he on top of Hollow Hill, beneath the old tree? It's where he likes to wait for people."

Angus tilted his head slightly and narrowed his eyes. "Aye, we did, lassie, that we did," he said and smiled an uncertain smile.

After a long, uncomfortable pause, another windy howl whooshed over the crackling logs. "Thanks again, Angus, my wife and I owe you and your friends a huge debt of gratitude. But now I think we all deserve a good night's sleep. After all, it is Christmas Eve tomorrow."

"Of course, I will take my leave. Sorry your new beginnings have been so troublesome, but give it a chance, we have a good community here."

Ameina stood and shook his hand. "I can see that. But if we do stay, we will need to move, I think."

"I understand, pity though, it's a beautiful hoose," offered the gamekeeper, before smoothing his yellow-grey hair over his head and pulling his deerstalker on tightly.

* * *

Eva watched her dad walk Angus towards the front door. She wanted to explain that Williwaw was not bad, Williwaw was really Boreas and he was searching for his daughter, *not* luring children out in the snow to take them away forever. Eva knew that if she had said anything about what Harry had told her, she would never have any chance of helping Boreas again.

As Angus reached for the door handle, he paused to face Tom. "There's something that's been bothering me, about what your daughter just said."

"Oh?"

"She mentioned us finding Harry, the Campbell's young boy."

"And?"

"Well, I never told her where we found him, how could she have known it was on Hollow Hill, beneath the tree?"

"She must have guessed. It sounds to me like she's already met the boy. I will ask her in the morning. Didn't you say the Campbell family moved somewhere local after they left this house?"

"Aye they did. But something I didn't mention: when we found Harry, he had sadly frozen to death..."

*　　*　　*

Within minutes of tucking her in, Eva had fallen into a deep sleep. Ameina watched over her for a little while longer before kissing her lightly and leaving the room. She climbed into her own bed and was thankful for Tom keeping it warm.

"I'm worried about Eva, I think she's really missing her friends. She would never have gone off like that back home, especially not alone," said Tom.

"I know, I feel terrible about it, I thought she would manage better. Change is easier for adults, but from a child's view, the world is a very different place and sometimes we forget that. I don't think she will disappear again like that. I will speak with her properly about it, but I think it best to wait until after Christmas."

They both lay together in thought, wondering if they could have handled things a little better, wondering if they had made the right choice to move.

"Tom."

"Yes, darling."

"There's something you should know."

"What is it?"

"How I knew you should go to a churchyard."

Tom sat up. "How *did* you know? I forgot about that."

"I feel crazy just hearing myself say it, but the truth is, as I watched you all disappear up the hill, the frost on the kitchen window... well, it formed the word 'churchyard' in front of my eyes..." Ameina looked down at the thick blanket and began pushing out the creases while her tears vanished into the soft material, leaving small dark spots.

"Hey, I believe you, it's been a crazy night for everyone."

She looked up and squeezed his hand. "How *can* you believe me, you weren't there."

"There's something I haven't told anyone else either. When we were trying to find a way into the churchyard, during the storm, somebody helped me."

"Who?"

"A small Scottish boy, he said his name was Harry."

Chapter Ten

"Hurry up, Dad's waiting in the car."

"Coming, Mum!" yelled Eva, pulling on her faux leather boots, enjoying the spongey warmth of the thick inner lining.

She ran past Mum locking the front door and slid along the slippery snow the car tyres had flattened. Panting, Eva turned to face the house, admiring its quirkiness through small puffs of warm air.

"Let's hope the local village has not run out of food, or we will be eating toast for Christmas dinner," joked Dad as he pulled away, carefully swinging the car into the narrow country lane. Fortunately, the farmer had already cleared the snow, and Tom made a mental note to thank him later for doing so.

For the rest of the drive Eva watched the icy wind whipping up freshly fallen flakes from the glittering snowdrifts, creating a breath-taking sparkly haze beneath the early sun. Mum and Dad were singing terribly out of tune to Christmas songs being played on the radio and Eva grinned despite the noise. Her thoughts returned to the last thing she had seen before she bumped her head in the graveyard. She recalled a soft light coming from the other side of the crypt gate. It had to be her, it had to be Snow. At least she knew where to find her and how to gain entry into the disused churchyard. She would wait until after Christmas before looking again; she didn't want to ruin anything her parents had planned, knowing she had caused quite enough trouble already.

"Here we are, City central! Well, Village central," joked Dad.

After leaving the car, Mum turned and clapped her hands. "Isn't it beautiful, sweetheart?"

Eva had to agree, especially when everything sparkled in the sun. "It's perfect, Mum."

The high-street was divided by a tall, stone, clock tower. Every side displayed a large, maroon, clock face, beset with gleaming, golden numerals. Beneath, proudly stood a huge Christmas tree dressed in purple and gold tinsel, with spiralling, soft-white fairy lights that flashed and faded.

"Your father and I will only be a few minutes in this shop. Why don't you take a look around, but *please* don't go far this time."

"I won't," said Eva. She knew they were buying Christmas surprises and she didn't want to spoil it for them.

For a place that seemed to be in the middle of nowhere, she was surprised at the amount of shops and busy people, all making last minute preparations before the big day. Every shop had been richly decorated, with customers chatting to shop owners, sampling their free food and drink, while a brass band collected money for charity by playing uplifting carols—thankfully in tune, despite wearing gloves. Familiar scents wafted through the air, warm cinnamon, spicy gingerbread, hot mince pies, and fresh pine needles. The smells and sights were a welcome distraction. Eva couldn't help surrendering herself to the Christmas spirit and giggled when an old man wearing a kilt danced beside a red-faced musician playing the tuba.

As Eva approached the last shop, the high-street became

a simple road again, deserted and empty. She was about to turn back, then heard a whistle. Shielding a hand against the sun's glare, she caught sight of someone waving behind a weathered granite wall on the opposite side of the road. Slowly she advanced, wary of who it might be, even though they seemed to know her.

"Harry!"

The small boy stood in a field surrounded by curious cattle, looking very distressed.

"What's wrong, is everything alright? What happened to you last night? You left me all alone."

"I'm sorry, Eva, I tried to go through the gate but I couldn't, I was too afraid..."

"Well, I was scared too, I almost died! If it hadn't been for Angus and his friends, who knows what might have happened to me?"

Harry looked down, kicking the snow and spoke quietly. "I know I left you, but I did get Boreas to tell your mum where to find you."

"What do you mean?"

"Boreas wrote churchyard on my kitchen window and your mum told everyone you were there," said Harry proudly.

Eva's eyes widened. "My mum knows about Boreas."

Harry looked up again shaking his head. "No! No, she doesn't know anything else, not about finding Snow, I promise."

"Good, because if she did I would not be able to help you anymore. After last night we will have to stop this for a while, at least until things return back to normal, maybe in the New Year?"

Dismayed, Harry ran over to her. "No! We *must* keep looking, we *have* to find her! Eva, if we don't, she will die."

"I know, you already told me this."

"Yes, but Boreas told me we only have one day left at

most. Because of last night's searching, nearly all the snow has gone and then it will be too late. She needs us, Eva, Snow needs us!"

Eva hopped over the short, stone wall and hugged Harry, while he cried into her coat. "My mum and dad will be mad with me and will probably ground me for the rest of my life, but I understand and I do want to help you. I promise I will find a way to leave the house later. At least we know exactly where to go now, it shouldn't take as long, I hope."

Harry looked into her eyes, his own shining with a strange light, and his small, crooked smile touched her heart. "You're the best friend anyone could ever wish for, Eva, thank you."

Eva's phone began ringing in her pocket. After some fumbling she pulled it out and checked the screen. "I have to leave now, it's my Mum an—"

By the time she looked up, Harry had vanished. She spun around but he was nowhere to be seen.

"That's twice you've done that to me, Harry Campbell!" snapped Eva jokingly, as she hurried back up the high-street, careful to not slip over. When she found her parents they looked relieved and heavily weighed down by several stuffed bags they both carried in each hand.

"Here, let me help."

"Um, that's a nice offer, poppet, but we can manage," said Mum, making sure Eva didn't peep inside them.

Eva grinned, trudging beside them through the thick slush.

"You, wait! You, yes you! You're the new girl, aren't you? Have you seen my Harry?" shouted a desperate-looking woman from across the street.

Before anyone could respond the woman ran over to them and was almost hit by a car.

Dad stood in front of Eva. "Who are you? What do you want with my daughter?" he demanded.

The woman straightened herself and scooped her untidy hair back, then coughed out a reply. "I need to speak with your daughter please, she knows where my son is!"

"Please, calm down. If you mean Harry Campbell, I fully understand why you are so upset and offer my sincerest sympathy, but what you are saying is quite impossible."

Eva nudged around to see the woman. She sounded deeply distressed and looked as though she hadn't slept in over a year. Her frantic eyes were set within large, black circles, sunken within her hollow face. Her clothes and hair were scruffy and she looked painfully thin.

"It's okay, Dad, let me talk to her."

"No, let me deal with this please. Are you Mrs Campbell?"

"Yes, yes I am," replied the woman thickly.

"You have probably heard that we have just moved into your old house, but that does not mean we know where your son is. I'm terribly sorry, but we cannot help you any further," said Tom compassionately, yet firmly.

"But your daughter? I heard your daughter had seen him, spoken with him," she replied, tears running down her gaunt face.

"Where did you hear this?"

"I overheard other folk talking, down at Fingle's Inn, saying that my son helped your daughter escape from Williwaw."

"Whatever you think you heard is wrong. My daughter strayed too far from home last night and was caught in a snow storm. We found her, thank God, but whatever happened to your son, we are truly sorry. Please do not ask us again as we know nothing more." Tom ushered his wife and daughter up the road, leaving the anguished woman and several other villagers looking after them.

"But, Dad—"

Tom stopped walking and bent down. He freed himself

of the plastic bags and held his daughter's hand. "Honey, I don't know who helped you last night, or who helped me in finding you, but that woman's son went missing too, just like you in a snowstorm, and his name was Harry Campbell. Sweetheart, Harry Campbell was found dead, frozen by the storm and that was over three years ago..."

Eva gasped and her hand went limp in her Dad's.

"I don't feel too well, can we go home now please?"

"Of course we can, honey," said Mum, shooting a worried look at Tom. "The car's just up here. What happened is all in the past, now we have Christmas to look forward to!"

Eva nodded, although she barely heard her mum talking. What did this all mean? Was it the same Harry? If it was, then how could a dead boy talk to her, touch her? No, he was real, he had to be.

After getting in the car, Dad put the heating on full. It didn't take long before she could remove her coat, but she still felt chilled to the bone, a chill that no amount of warmth would reach. What if Harry was a ghost, a real ghost? Eva pulled her coat back on and buried herself within its cushioned layers. Well, he wasn't a scary ghost, she supposed, just a sad and frightened one. The more Eva reasoned with what she knew, the more she realised she needn't be afraid, at least not of Harry. But what if it was a trap after all? What if Boreas was really a bad spirit and lied about having a daughter who made snow so he could steal children away from their parents? Whatever the truth was about Snow, Harry still needed Eva's help. He came to *her* and no one else and if he *was* a ghost, then he was trapped here and needed to be freed, to go where everyone went when they died, to go to heaven, Eva presumed.

It was decided. Eva was determined to find out the truth of the matter. She wasn't afraid, she knew where to go and how to get there. Harry was her new friend and she wouldn't leave him when he needed her the most.

Chapter Eleven

After Dad had lifted up Eva to place a magnificent gold star on the top of the tree, they all stood back to admire its glittering brilliance.

Eva was glad they had brought the old Christmas tree with them. Mum had always refused to cut down a perfectly healthy tree, so Dad had bought an artificial one. They had it for as long as she could remember and it made their new place feel like home. It looked a little shabby now and two of the branches were missing, but she felt happy just looking at it.

"Stop staring and get moving. You're the tall one, these decorations aren't going to hang themselves!" chided Mum with a grin.

Dad sighed, opening another cardboard box, armed with sticky tape and a rickety step ladder, which was covered in blobs of dried paint in every colour imaginable.

Eva felt terrible but she had no choice. Harry had warned her how little time they had. If she couldn't find Snow in time then winter would be nothing more than cold, wet darkness. And what of Christmas? She couldn't imagine a world where it no longer snowed, where children couldn't go sledging with their families, or make snowmen, or throw snowballs. What would happen to all the winter sports, or the environment? How would the world change if it didn't snow anymore? It was all down to her. No one could possibly understand her, or believe her, but if this was all real then she *had* to help.

Eva suddenly realised she was much stronger than she first believed. She now felt able to face this enormous challenge alone, without any help from the friends she had left behind. She knew she could do this, she *would* do this, for Harry's sake and for Snow.

"I'm just going for a hot bath if that's okay, Mum?"

"Sure, that's fine, honey, I will call you when tea's ready."

Dad was busy sticking up the same piece of tinsel several times while complaining beneath his breath, as Eva walked out of the living room. She ran quietly over to the front door where she had left her scarf and gloves on a hot radiator. Silently, she tugged on her warm boots and zipped up her thick, burgundy jacket. Searching inside the pocket, she felt the torch she had put there earlier. Carefully, Eva opened the front door and instantly a harsh wind pulled on it. She walked outside and eased the door shut again waiting for a click. Satisfied no one had heard, she crunched slowly around the side of the house towards the back garden. She had checked from inside the house that nothing could be seen outside the frosted windows. Only fairy lights and the fire's glow reflected back in the glass, creating a strange and magical winter's scene where the garden should have been.

Keeping hidden from sight, Eva crept down the side of the garden waiting for her name to be called out; thankfully it wasn't. When she had made it safely to the old gate at the bottom of the garden, she wiped away the snow and pushed down on the gate latch, but it wouldn't budge. Looking down, Eva could see the snow had piled up, stopping it from opening, so she kicked away enough to try again. Gradually it edged open, allowing her to squeeze through. When she had made it far enough up the hill to be safe from view, Eva took out her torch and fumbled with it until the light came on, although it was a clear night and the moon was enough to see by.

"Hi!"

Eva jumped with surprise. Sitting atop the hill beneath the knobbly yew tree was Harry, grinning mischievously.

"Harry! I wondered when I might see you again," replied Eva, nervous and awkward looking.

"What's wrong, have I done something to upset you?"

"No. It's just something my dad said earlier today, it doesn't matter. What matters now is that we need to keep moving, my parents will know I've gone missing again."

"I'm sorry, I don't want you to get into any trouble, but I can't do this alone," he replied, in that little, lost boy way he did so often.

She studied him closely; he certainly looked and sounded normal enough. Instead of fearing him, Eva felt sorry for him. "Don't you worry, Harry, we will do this together, tonight..."

*   *   *

"You're not going to believe this, the wee girl we rescued last night has gone missing again."

Angus choked on his drink. "Are you sure, Dougall?"

"Aye, it was that Tom calling, says his daughter has taken her coat and boots and left the house again. Says she might have gone back to the churchyard, as the back gate to his garden was left open."

After wiping the frothy ale from his beard and jumper, Angus spoke. "Not again and not on Christmas Eve, of all nights." He stood up and quietened down the music. "Right, finish up your drinks and meals, ladies and gentleman, we have another bairn ta find!"

Chapter Twelve

As Eva and Harry turned the corner, the wind thrashed and shrieked around them, covering them in heavy, wet snowflakes. The weather had taken a sudden and dramatic turn for the worse, after they had begun their descent of Hollow Hill. Several times they heard Boreas on the wind, calling out his daughter's name, encouraging the brave pair to venture onwards. His despairing voice was full of sadness, knowing his own presence hindered their search and endangered his own daughter's life; yet without him, Snow would never have the strength to return back to her home world, if they ever managed to find her.

"Here it is!" yelled the small, pale boy, pointing to where a curtain of ivy swung about wildly.

Eva shone her torch over, catching a dull glint of iron hidden behind it.

After heaving it open, Eva stepped through. "C'mon, Harry, I know where she is, follow me!"

Harry shook his head, "Sorry, I can't go in there, I tried last time, but I saw things, things that scared me, unnatural things."

"I didn't see anything like that, it's just a churchyard with old graves." Eva could see the look of fear on Harry's face, then suddenly she realised. Harry could see things she could not. He didn't know he was a ghost, he was stuck between worlds, stuck in a constant search for Snow, and could probably see other ghosts haunting the graveyard.

"It's okay, Harry, why don't you wait here for me? Try to keep out of the storm though, I will be as quick as I can."

Harry nodded and hid behind a rusted sheep pen made from corrugated iron, with a loose end that kept banging in the wind.

As Eva entered the churchyard, it felt like she hadn't left. Everything was exactly how she remembered it the night before, only the storm was worse. Holding out her torch, she could see the floor a little better and made her way towards the area she thought the crypt to be. Every now and then, she felt a powerful gust of wind steer her a little to the left or right. Sensing it was Boreas helping her, she went with it.

The snowfall was now so thick, a couple of times Eva choked trying to breathe. She felt a sickening sense of fear beginning to creep in. *You can do this, you must do this, no one else can help but you,* she kept telling herself, as she stumbled onwards, struggling to move against the icy blasts. Somewhere in the blizzard Eva caught sight of a faint silvery glow, it had to be Snow! With renewed hope, she found the strength to carry on, until eventually she stood at the steps that led down into the crypt. This time she sat down upon the icy steps and slowly made her way to the bottom where the iron gates stood.

Even though only ten foot below ground level, the weather was considerably more bearable and Eva could now see and breathe without having to shield her face. Peering through the iron bars, Eva could make out a pulsing light; it was faint but it *was* there.

"Snow! Can you hear me? I'm taking you back to your home, to Hyperborea."

Eva strained to hear a reply but heard nothing. Moving aside clumps of frozen creepers, she pushed down on the handle, but the gate was locked with a padlock.

"Snow! How do I get in? I can't get in! Please, somebody help me..." she cried, rattling the gate with all of her strength, but it was useless. Eva sat slumped against the bars sobbing, knowing she had failed. What was she thinking, that she alone could save Snow without the help from any of her friends? She wished she was back home now with them, she missed them so much and wondered if she would ever see them again.

"Evaaaa... looocck..."

She opened her eyes, wiping the blurriness away. What did Boreas mean? Her heart skipped a beat as the padlock on the gate completely froze over with frost; so much so, it turned blue!

"Puuuushhh..."

She jumped up and pushed the gate with everything she had...

"Clunk!"

The padlock fell to the ground and shattered. Eva swung the gate wide open with a grinding creak. "Thank you, Boreas, thank you!" she yelled and ran inside.

* * *

"I feel terrible for asking but I don't know what else to do," said Tom, grabbing his coat.

"It's nay bother, it's good ta get out of that stuffy inn and get some fresh air back into my lungs," replied Angus, stomping his feet and rubbing his hands.

"Does it usually snow like this?"

"In all my years I have never seen it so bad, which is why we didn't hesitate helping your family. If she's ta stand any chance out there, she going ta need every last one of us."

"Bless you all, I don't know how to repay you. I have no idea what's gotten into her, she always tells us when she goes out and where she's going," said Ameina, changing the batteries in the spare torch.

"No, I think you should stay put, just in case she comes home," said Tom.

"No, Tom, she's my daughter too. If she's lost out there in this weather then I'm coming to help!"

Tom looked into her eyes and knew she would not change her mind.

"Don't worry, if it's okay with you I can ask Mary if she will stay here, just in case the wee lass does return home. Mary lives down the lane, we are old friends. She may be as tough as ol' boots, but she cannae go fadoodling in this weather at her age," offered Angus.

Ameina nodded her approval. "Thank you, that would be a great help, Angus."

*　　*　　*

Eva banged her torch a couple of times. Its beam was beginning to dim. She continued walking towards the glow somewhere within the crypt, aware the further she walked away from the howling winds, the louder her gritty footsteps became upon the cold, bare, marble floor. She could see the peculiar light coming from beneath a large metal door, displaying a wooden placard with "Burial Vault" written in gold lettering upon it, which was peeling with age.

"Snow, are you in there?" she called, hearing her voice trail around the empty chamber. There was no reply.

Eva's heart raced; something *was* inside and it was waiting for her to open the door. She placed a shaky hand upon the handle and took a last look around at the eerie marble chamber, as her failing torchlight allowed more shadowy creatures to leap into view. Turning the handle, Eva half expected a ghoul or hideous monster to jump out, but to her relief and surprise, the door opened easily and silently.

Saving Snow

Taking a deep breath, she walked over the threshold and saw the silver light immediately. It was much brighter and shining from the far side of the burial chamber.

Fortunately, she didn't need to dodge any hungry rats, or kick aside dusty skeletons, the burial chamber had been maintained respectfully well. Hesitant, she edged towards the strange light. It was partially concealed behind a raised stone plinth next to the far wall.

"Snow... is that you...?" croaked Eva, excited and afraid.

She jumped as the heavy door slammed shut behind her. Ahead she saw the light shifting and with it, a small scraping noise. Eva was ready to run, every part of her trembling with anticipation.

"Hello, is somebody there?" replied a weak but gentle voice.

Pushing aside her fear, Eva ran over to the other side of the plinth and gasped. In front of her sat a girl bathed in platinum light, who looked about the same age, with beautiful, long silver hair that shimmered. Her skin also sparkled, like thousands of tiny diamonds, and her sorrowful eyes were like two full moons, grey and luminous. She sat cradling herself, wrapped in a silvery dress, looking confused and lost.

"Snow, I've found you! How did you become trapped in *here*?"

After examining Eva's face, she pointed high up towards some small windows. One of the windows had a small piece of glass missing, no larger than her thumb.

"Did you fall through there, when you were a snowflake?"

Snow nodded and tried to smile.

"We don't have much time, your father searches for you and hasn't stopped searching ever since you vanished. Boreas misses you terribly and he says that without you there can be no more snow in our world because all the snow coming from your world has nearly run out."

Kneeling on the marble floor, Eva removed her own coat and placed it around the frail girl. Snow smiled and shook her head.

"I do not feel the cold as you do, but thank you."

Surprised by her response, Eva took back her coat and laughed awkwardly.

"Sorry, I wasn't thinking. My name's Eva, I'm a friend of Harry, do you know him?"

Snow shook her head and tried to get up, but she was too weak.

Eva supported her and helped her on to her feet.

"Thank you, Eva. I never thought anyone would come for me. I have grown so tired these past years. I could sense my father close many times, but even if he heard me call out to him, he could not help me. It's the snow that keeps us strong in your world, but the more he searches, the less snow there is left and together we have grown very weak."

"Harry, the boy I mentioned, told me about this and that we only have today left to save you. What does that mean exactly, what will happen?"

"It means the last snowflake will soon fall and when it lands there will be no more..."

"And what of you and Boreas?"

Snow looked into Eva's eyes; a single sparkling teardrop fell and she looked down.

"Well, that's not going to happen! Take my hand."

Eva put her arm around Snow's waist and helped her towards the door. It wasn't difficult, Snow barely weighed anything and Eva had to check several times she was actually holding her at all. Eva turned the handle but the door wouldn't open. She tugged it harder but it was firmly locked shut.

"Oh no, the door is locked. Maybe it can only be opened from the other side?"

Eva knew it was pointless asking Snow about any other way to escape; she had been trapped in the burial chamber for years. Despair and panic rose within Eva and she choked back the tears. But her parents knew she was found at the crypt yesterday; hopefully they would come again and they would see the gate open. But what if they found them too late and the last snowflake had landed?

"I am so sorry, Snow, I tried, I really tried—"

Snow held a finger to her lips and craned her head to listen. Eva stopped talking and listened too. It sounded as if someone was on the other side of the door. They both held their breath as the door handle suddenly began to turn.

Chapter Thirteen

The Campbell child looked every bit as relieved as the two girls, theatrically holding the door open as they walked through, despite his cautious eyes darting to every flinching shadow he saw.

"I felt terrible watching you walk away by yourself. I wouldn't be much of a friend if I didn't help you, not after asking for your help in the first place."

"I know how much courage it took you, Harry. You are a true friend."

Harry grinned and jumped for joy when he looked at Snow. "You're real! I have been looking for you all night. Your dad has been worried sick."

Eva looked away, she couldn't face Harry. His parents had missed him for so long and he didn't even know. Harry believed he had been out for only a few hours searching for Snow, when really it had been three long years.

"What's wrong, Eva? Are you okay? C'mon, we have to take Snow back to her dad."

"It's alright, Harry, it's just dusty in here," she smiled.

As they helped Snow through the silent crypt, Snow faltered and her light began to flicker.

"Snow, what's happening?"

The frail girl pointed towards the crypt gates. "We must

hurry..." she murmured, barely able to open her eyes.

After dragging Snow free of the crypt, Eva gasped in dismay. Although the winds were fierce and a deep build-up of fresh snow had fallen, the dwindling snowflakes were now all but gone. The winds whipped around the graveyard in a frenzy, whisking large ribbons of twinkling, settled snow high into the air, but above this, in the pinkish brooding sky, the last few remaining flakes toppled down.

"Father..."

"Snowwww, I'm heeeeere..."

For a brief moment, a faded image of Boreas came into view—a huge bearded man with kind eyes and hair the colour of storm clouds.

"What's wrong? We found Snow for you. Why don't you take her back?" demanded Harry, visibly shaking with tears streaming down his colourless cheeks.

"Harry, they have become too weak to help each other. We are too late, I don't know what else to do," said Eva, holding her head in her hands.

"Go... tooo... Holowwww..."

"Hollow? Hollow! Harry, help me take Snow to Hollow Hill, there might still be time!"

Together they raced as fast as they could, struggling through the deep, freezing snow. Eva couldn't shake the thought it might be the last time she would ever see it.

*　*　*

"Aye, she's been here alright, this gate was secured last night and goodness knows how the lock's been shattered like this," said Angus, scratching his head.

"Angus, there's no one inside. I checked everywhere, almost got locked in the vault for doing so!" shouted McKenzie, squeezing back through the gates.

"Look! Two pairs of footprints are going down the steps

and three pairs are coming back up," said the old gamekeeper, slicking back his damp hair before pulling his hat back on tightly.

"Are you sure, Angus? Who could possibly be with my daughter? Maybe one of the search team?" questioned Tom, a trace of hope in his voice.

"No. If it was one of us we would all know about it by now. Besides, all these footprints are small, children's, I would wager. The only thing we can do for now is follow the footprints and hope we can catch up with them. Thankfully the snow has all but stopped, but this wind is chilling me ta the bare bones."

Chapter Fourteen

"I don't know why Boreas told us to go to Hollow Hill, what difference will it make?" complained Harry.

Eva could barely reply; her mouth was painfully dry and she was utterly exhausted. "Maybe... maybe Boreas has... a plan?" she replied, little more than a whisper.

Often the brave rescuers would stumble and fall, but Boreas would immediately help them back up by blowing powerful gusts of icy wind at their backs. Eva became sleepy, the cold had reached into every part and her body felt numb and heavy, yet still they continued to fight their way towards the impossible summit, urged on by Boreas.

When Eva thought she could not go on, Harry stopped and shouted, "Look, up there!"

"It's the last snowflake..." sighed Snow, as they watched it dance alone, high in the sky.

It was brilliant silver with a halo of white fire that blazed brightly. In a blinding flash Eva knew exactly what she must do. She faced the others and tried to speak but her mouth was too dry. Scooping up some snow, Eva rubbed her cracked lips, "We have to get Snow to the last flake before it lands, we still have a chance."

From somewhere deep within, Eva found a burst of

energy and together they marched up the unforgiving incline, becoming closer and closer to the top. Eva believed Boreas had known all along what he was doing when he had sent them to Hollow Hill. He must have seen the last flake falling from the clouds, heading towards the hillside, and then kept it afloat for as long as he was able to, enough for Snow to catch it before it landed.

"What are those lights, Eva?" panted Harry.

Eva looked over her shoulder and saw dozens of torch beams shining up the hill behind them.

"It must be my parents, they've come out looking for me. We can't stop for anyone, not even for them, Harry."

She felt terribly guilty about all the good people risking their lives searching for her, and felt worse for her parents. They didn't deserve this, she knew how hard life had been for them recently. Eva knew they missed their old home just as much as she had and how they had to leave their friends as well.

*   *   *

Angus studied the footprints and could see they were freshly made. "Tom, Ameina, I think we are close. These footprints are new, we are very close indeed."

"Angus! Look up the hill, I see a strange light, do you see it too?" yelled Dougall, straining to see through the wind-whipped snowdrifts.

"Aye, I do, what is that...?"

"I have no idea, but I'm not waiting to find out, Eva may be in trouble," replied Tom, striding past everyone until he was out in front. He paused, then looked behind at Ameina.

"Go, Tom, I will be right behind you!"

*   *   *

74

Saving Snow

The silver flake fluttered dangerously low in the sky, spinning and twirling around. Despite Boreas's best efforts, it was still drifting lower and lower. The children were only a short way from the hilltop where the yew tree stood proudly, its vast silhouette dominating the night sky. At the last few steps, Snow stumbled and the children all fell down together, sprawled beneath the crooked, swaying branches. Utterly exhausted, they watched helplessly as the silver flake floated towards them. Snow raised her arm weakly and stretched out her hand, but it wasn't enough...

The last snowflake had already landed, perched upon a branch and out of reach.

Harry slumped to the ground staring upwards and cried.

Looking into Snow's mournful eyes, Eva could see her inner light was fading. Her fragile body had lost its sparkle and swiftly became shadowy and see-through. For the first time, Eva felt coldness grow within Snow's body and held her close. "I'm sorry, Snow, I didn't want it to end this way, I tried my best, really I did, please, *please* don't die..."

Eva began to cry too; this wasn't fair, none of this was. What had been the point to any of this, if it had to end in this way? They all lay huddled together, watching the last flake settle, its silvery light dying as fast as Snow was. *If only I could reach it!* thought Eva.

She pulled off her glove and felt the air. The wind had all but vanished, but there was still a faint draught.

"Boreas! Boreas! I know you can hear me. If you have anything left in you, please use it to blow the snowflake down. You can do this, we believe in you..."

Eva stood clumsily, carrying Snow in her arms, who had all but vanished and felt lighter than air. Positioning Snow beneath the branch, they waited and prayed.

Somewhere within his failing mind, Boreas heard their prayers. He roused himself enough to gather in the very last of his essence, but only enough for one final gust of wind, knowing he would then disappear forever, "Forrrr... myyy... Snowwww..."

They held their breath and watched as the branch swayed just a little. Now almost invisible, the tiny flake wavered between the dense pine needles, then gently tugged itself loose. Eva took Snow's hand in hers and quickly held it beneath the very last snowflake...

"Eva! Eva!"

She spun around and saw her father clambering up the hill. She was about to call out but a sudden flash of blinding light exploded in her arms. She looked back and caught her breath. Snow was now holding Eva, wearing a beaming smile. She had never seen Snow shine like this; her hair, her body, those beautiful moonlike eyes, all dazzled a brilliant silver.

"Don't be afraid, you are safe. Do you believe in magic now, Eva?"

Eva felt weightless and looked around. She was somehow floating high in the air. It seemed as though night had become day, so intense was Snow's radiance. Nervously, Eva peered downwards and could see her mum and dad standing with all the villagers. They were shielding their eyes from the brightness.

"You're saved! We saved you!"

"You saved me, Eva, *you* saved snow."

In that moment Eva felt such joy and happiness, as if bringing snow back to the world had brought back all the love. As they hugged, Boreas came into view, with the kindest smile she had ever seen.

"You didn't give up on us, Eva, this I will never forget. I sensed your heavy heart, you felt so alone, but you are never alone, child. The love you hold in your heart for someone is more real than anything else in this world, or any other world. Whenever you feel alone, think of someone with your heart and they will be there with you, inside that love."

Boreas touched Eva's chest lightly and she felt a small jolt of electricity run through her. A glow spread over her body and she felt all the coldness leave her.

"We must return to our home world, Eva, we have been gone too long, but we are now connected to you. Think of us in your heart and you will never feel alone or cold again."

"I will never forget you, Snow, Boreas."

Eva began floating back down. "Snow! What about Harry? What about his mum and dad?" she shouted, shielding her eyes against the light.

Harry instantly appeared and held Eva's hand as they both returned back to the ground.

"Sweetheart, you are safe, we were worried so, so much for you..." cried Mum, as Eva's parents clutched their daughter tightly, so tight that Eva struggled to breathe.

"It's okay, Mum, Dad, really it is. I hope you will forgive me. I couldn't tell you what was happening because you wouldn't have let me help."

"Who are they? Where are they from? Did they harm you?" asked Mum, staring upwards in disbelief.

"No. They just needed my help. That's Snow and that's her father, Boreas. They come from another world. It's why I sneaked out, Snow was dying here and I had to save her, with Harry's help."

"But, Sweetheart, that's not possible, Harry's..."

"A ghost, I know," grinned Eva proudly.

A frantic couple pushed past the villagers. "Harry, Harry, is that really you?"

Harry had a huge smile when he saw his parents. He had lost his confused, anxious expression and now looked at peace with himself. "Mum, Dad, yes, it's—"

Before he could finish, Mrs. Campbell fell to her knees and pulled him close, kissing all over his face, and didn't stop, fearful she might awaken from a dream. Finally, she moved away, shrinking inside herself. "But, you're not real, I saw your body, how is it I can feel you?" She collapsed and wept.

Harry walked over in silence; everyone else was too shocked to do or say anything other than watch. He bent down, taking his mother's hand in his. "Mum, I'm as real as you are. I'm sorry for leaving you and Dad, but you must stop crying for me. Instead be happy, happy that I'm not really gone, I'm just moving on to somewhere else, where hopefully it's a bit warmer."

Harry's dad kneeled down beside his wife and together they hugged as a family for the last time, until they would all meet again.

"You can feel me, Mum, because you're feeling with your heart and not your hands, silly. Eva will tell you the same, all you need to do to feel someone is search within your heart for the love you hold and they will be right there with you. I will always be there with you, because I will always live in your hearts."

"I feel it, Harry, it feels like bursting. I love you so much, we both do, please don't leave us again."

"I have to go, but it won't be for long, you'll see. I will wait for you both in the next place."

Harry's dad held his mum while she wept. She nodded and kissed her son's hand, watching it leave hers. Harry gently lifted off the ground to return next to Snow and Boreas.

The three of them stood smiling, waved and turned to walk towards a golden doorway, suspended in the night sky.

As they entered, Boreas turned and spoke. "Don't you all have some preparations to be getting on with? Merry Christmas to all and a Happy New Year!" His voice boomed across the land like a thunder clap and his deep laughter could still be heard long after they had vanished from sight.

Angus stood with his mouth open in shock, quite unable

to move, as did the other villagers.

Eva ran over to him and tugged on his coat. "Angus, are you alright? Say something, please!"

"Williwaw just wished me a Merry Christmas..."

Eva and her parents couldn't help but laugh, as Angus gazed upwards, unblinking and utterly astonished.

After everyone had shared their incredible experiences—to make sure they were not imagining things—the dazed villagers wished each other well and returned to the warmth of their homes. When Eva arrived back at her house, her parents decided to leave the rest of the decorating until the morning. The Christmas tree was already up and that was quite enough for now. There were many, many questions that still needed answering, but completely exhausted they all fell into their beds, with a fading thought of what the next day might bring, knowing now that anything was possible.

Chapter Fifteen

A n odd noise awoke Eva. It sounded like hundreds of ice skaters, skating slowly. Heavy-eyed, she peeped above the top of her blankets towards the window where it was coming from. Gingerly, she placed a foot out of bed searching for a slipper and feeling grateful that Dad had set the heating to come on early. After her toe found it, she wriggled into its woolly warmth and did the same for the other foot. Pushing aside the thick bedding, Eva yawned as she walked over to the heavy, velvet curtains and pulled them apart, stopping mid yawn. Her windows were covered in beautiful frost ferns, sparkling brightly in the morning sun. In the centre, like before, was an oval space left untouched, where she could still peer out from.

"Mum, Dad, quick, look outside!"

*   *   *

Tom groaned and rubbed his eyes. "What time is it, have we missed Christmas?"

Ameina giggled and checked the clock on her bedside table, "No, but it looks like we're up now, so Happy Christmas, husband," she said, grabbing her dressing gown before running over to the window.

"Tom, quickly, look outside!"

"This had better be worth leaving my cosy bed for," he muttered, hauling himself out.

"What in the..."

It had been snowing again that night, at least another foot deep, but this time every flake was iridescent, as if the snowflakes had fallen through a rainbow. As far as they could see, everywhere shimmered in bright, flickering, multi coloured sparkles.

"It's incredible, its—"

"It's Boreas and Snow!" cried Eva, running into their bedroom, throwing her arms around them.

*   *   *

"Happy Christmas, sweetheart," said Mum and Dad.

"Happy Christmas, it's the best one ever," exclaimed Eva.

The three of them ran downstairs to get a better look. After grabbing coats and pulling on boots, they spilled outside from the back door to gaze in wonderment.

"Mum, it's so pretty, I have never seen anything so beautiful..." breathed Eva.

She smiled, watching her parents' confusion develop into excited grins. By the look of them, Eva reckoned her parents were remembering what it felt like to be children again.

"Eva, where's your coat? You will freeze, darling," said Mum.

Eva looked down. She was standing in just her pyjamas and yet she could not feel the cold at all; if anything she felt warmer.

"Mum, Dad, something's different, something's changed! I can't feel the cold anymore."

"You've probably got a slight fever or something. After

the past few days it's hardly surprising," said Dad, bending down to feel his daughter's temperature.

"That's strange, your body feels cold, not hot. How do you feel, Eva?"

"I feel amazing." she replied, giggling as her dad's confusion returned.

"Is that your phone, Tom?" said Mum, looking back towards the house.

Dad ran inside, leaving them to enjoy the incredible scene.

After a couple of minutes, Tom yelled for them both to come back inside.

"Tom, what is it?" asked Ameina worriedly.

"Quick, look at the television."

After kicking off their boots, they half jumped back into their slippers and shuffled over to the television.

"It's happening all over the world..." choked Dad.

"What is? What's happening?"

"The same multi-coloured snow is falling everywhere, like rainbow flakes falling from the skies. Hey, it's even snowing in Africa! How is that possible?" blurted Tom, shaking his head in disbelief.

Nearly every television channel they switched on was an emergency news broadcast. The screen kept jumping to news reporters from different countries, all filming the extraordinary, kaleidoscopic snowflakes floating down. Eva laughed as a news reporter stood shaking in the cold, pointing a trembling finger towards a snow-capped pyramid in Egypt.

"This is incredible, Tom..." said Mum, unable to look away from the television screen.

"It's a miracle, Ameina, a real Christmas miracle and it's all thanks to our little Eva."

Eva fell into an armchair as the shock hit her. She looked up at her parents. They were right. It didn't matter how she felt it about, the simple fact was, if she hadn't found the courage to help Boreas and Harry, none of this would have ever happened.

"Shhh, turn the sound down, Tom, what's that noise?" said Mum, tilting her head towards the front door.

"It sounds like singing and lots of laughter. The phone call I had was from Angus, he told me to switch on the television, I bet he's coming—" Before Tom could finish, there was a loud rapping on the front door.

"Eva, I think you had better get this," said Mum, as tears of joy she could no longer contain fell freely.

"Don't look so worried, poppet, it's just some new friends you have," grinned Dad.

Slowly, Eva got up and walked to the front hallway. She paused to look back then continued. Peering through the amber glass she couldn't make anything out, other than a dark, shifting shadow. Cautiously, she turned the latch and opened the door.

"Merry Christmas, Eva!" bellowed the old gamekeeper and lifted her high into the air amidst cheers and praises.

"Angus, merry Christmas to you, too."

"We couldna let you fine people have your day all ta yourselves now, could we? So the whole village thought it would be a splendid way ta greet you properly if we all spent Christmas together, down at Fingle's Inn. What do you reckon, lassie?"

"Yes, yes, can we, Dad? Please say yes, Mum?"

"We would be honoured," said Mum.

"Give us ten minutes to get ready, Angus. In the meantime, please come in and make yourselves welcome. As usual my wife has bought enough mince pies to feed an entire village; just as well I suppose," laughed Tom.

"Och no, there's far too many of us out here, we'd never fit. Besides, who wants ta stay inside when you can see a real, live fairy-tale outside?" replied Angus, giving Eva a big wink.

After Eva and her parents were dressed and left the house, the villagers cheered and clapped loudly. Eva was raised onto the gamekeeper's shoulders and quickly brought back down after his bandy legs almost gave out. The other villagers were already celebrating Christmas morning at Fingle's Inn, feeding logs to the fire and singing carols of old while waiting for the others to arrive.

Holding her parents' hands, they sang as they walked, bursting with cheer. Eva still missed her friends terribly and even though they had finally called her phone to wish her a happy Christmas, she still longed for their company. But she had learnt they were always with her, like Snow, Boreas and Harry, all within her heart. A memory suddenly filled her mind, of when she had held Snow as the last snowflake landed. Something had passed between them, something *had* changed her.

"Think of me whenever you feel lost or alone and I will be with you, Eva..." whispered a soft voice, carried upon the morning breeze.

Eva instantly looked up. Her parents hadn't heard it, only she had. It was Snow's voice! That was why she no longer felt the cold, because Snow was now a part of her.

"Mum, Dad, I have to do something."

Eva left her parents before they could question her and ran into the singing crowd. She slowed down when she saw Harry's mum. She looked different, as if a heavy weight had been lifted from off her shoulders. Now smiling, she held her head up a little higher as she walked. Eva ran over and took her hand.

"Can I walk with you for a while?" said Eva.

Without warning, Harry's mum swept her up into her arms. "Of course you can, I would like that a lot. We never had a chance to thank you properly, for what you did in helping our son, for helping us." Harry's mum struggled to speak further, but gone was the distant look that had haunted her face; now her bright, blue eyes sparkled like ice crystals captured in the early sunlight.

"You don't have to thank me, really you don't. Harry helped *me*. He showed me how to be brave when I thought I had no one, because all of us are never truly alone. Even when we think we can't go on and all hope is gone. Hope is everywhere, Mrs. Campbell, it's inside everyone and if ours runs out, well, we just need to borrow a bit from someone else until we find our way again."

"Thank you for lending me yours, Eva. Do you think, only if you want to of course, that from time to time your parents would let you come over for tea? Only if you want to?"

"I would like that, Mrs. Campbell, I would like that a lot."

Eva's parents re-joined her and together they all walked down the country lane in the morning sun. It was a Christmas they would never forget, a Christmas the whole world would never forget. Eva walked with pride, knowing she had finally figured out what the miracle of Christmas really was.

Quite simply, the miracle was *love*.

The End

"Thank you for reading Saving Snow. Gaining exposure as a new author relies mostly on word-of-mouth, so if you have the time and inclination, please consider leaving a short review on Amazon or wherever you can."

Printed in Great
Britain
by Amazon